# THE FUTURE IS BLACK

*The Future is Black* presents Afropessimism as an opportunity to think in provocative and disruptive ways about race, racial equality, multiculturalism, and the pursuit of educational justice. The vision is not a coherent, delimited conversation, but a series of experiences with Afropessimism as a radical analytic situated within critical Black studies. Activists, educators, caregivers, kin, and all those who love Black children are invited to make sense of the contemporary Black condition, including a theorization of Black suffering, Black fugitivity, and Black futurity. These three concepts provide the foundation for the book's inquiry, and contribute to the examination of Black educational opportunity, experience, and outcomes. The book not only explores how schooling becomes complicit in, and serves as, a site of Black material and psychic suffering but also examines the possibilities of education as a site of fugitivity, *of hope*, of escape, and as a space within which to imagine an emancipation yet to be realized.

**Carl A. Grant** is Hoefs-Bascom Professor of Education at the University of Wisconsin-Madison.

**Ashley N. Woodson** is the Stauffer Endowed Assistant Professor of Learning, Teaching and Curriculum at the University of Missouri-Columbia.

**Michael J. Dumas** is an Assistant Professor in the Graduate School of Education and Department of African American Studies at the University of California, Berkeley.

# THE FUTURE IS BLACK

Afropessimism, Fugitivity, and
Radical Hope in Education

*Edited by*
*Carl A. Grant,*
*Ashley N. Woodson, and*
*Michael J. Dumas*

Routledge
Taylor & Francis Group

NEW YORK AND LONDON

First published 2021
by Routledge
52 Vanderbilt Avenue, New York, NY 10017

and by Routledge
2 Park Square, Milton Park, Abingdon, Oxon, OX14 4RN

*Routledge is an imprint of the Taylor & Francis Group, an informa business*

© 2021 Taylor & Francis

*Library of Congress Cataloging-in-Publication Data*
Names: Grant, Carl A., editor. | Woodson, Ashley, editor. | Dumas,
Michael (Michael J.)
Title: The future is Black : Afropessimism, fugitivity, and radical hope
in education / edited by Carl A. Grant, Ashley Woodson, and Michael
Dumas.
Description: New York, NY : Routledge, 2019. |
Includes bibliographical references and index.
Identifiers: LCCN 2018060420| ISBN 9780815358190
(hbk : alk. paper) | ISBN 9780815358206 (pbk : alk. paper) |
ISBN 9781351122986 (ebk)
Subjects: LCSH: African Americans—Education—Social aspects. |
African Americans—Race identity. | Educational equalization—
United States.
Classification: LCC LC2717 .F87 2019 | DDC 378.1/982996073—dc23
LC record available at https://lccn.loc.gov/2018060420

ISBN: 978-0-8153-5819-0 (hbk)
ISBN: 978-0-8153-5820-6 (pbk)
ISBN: 978-1-351-12298-6 (ebk)

Typeset in Bembo
by codeMantra

# CONTENTS

# NOTES ON CONTRIBUTORS

## Editors

**Carl A. Grant** is the Hoefs-Bascom Professor in the Department of Curriculum and Instruction and former Chair of the Afro-American Studies Department at the University of Wisconsin-Madison. *Du Bois and Education* (2018) is his latest book.

**Ashley N. Woodson** is a mother, othermother and counterstoryteller who studies Black kids' civic imaginations and possibility. She is currently the William A. and Jean S. Stauffer Faculty Fellow in Education and an Assistant Professor at the University of Missouri-Columbia. She is currently listening to Patti LaBelle.

**Michael J. Dumas** is an Assistant Professor at the University of California, Berkeley in the Graduate School of Education and the African American Studies Department. He is primarily interested in how schools become sites of Black material and psychic suffering and anti-black violence, how disgust with and disdain for blackness inform defenses of inequitable distribution of educational resources, and ways that anti-blackness persists in education policy discourses and in broader public discourses on the worth of economic and educational investment in Black children.

## Chapter Authors

**Anthony L. Brown** is professor of social studies education and African and African diaspora studies at The University of Texas at Austin. His research explores (1) how education stakeholders understand and respond to Black male students and (2) how official and popular curriculum depict the historical experiences of Black Americans.

**Keffrelyn D. Brown** is professor of cultural studies in education and African and African diaspora studies at The University of Texas at Austin. Her research examines (1) the sociocultural knowledge of race in teaching, curriculum and teacher education, and (2) discourses and practices that shape Black intellectual thought and education.

**Erika C. Bullock** is an assistant professor at the University of Wisconsin-Madison. She historicizes issues and ideologies within mathematics and STEM education, examining how these disciplines create and maintain inequities. Her work has been published in *Educational Studies, Review of Research in Education* and *Teachers College Record* and featured in *The Atlantic*.

**Roderick L. Carey** is an assistant professor in the Department of Human Development and Family Sciences at the University of Delaware. He researches the ways Black and Latino adolescent boys, who live and learn within urban contexts, imagine and enact their postsecondary futures given both family and school influences.

**T. Elon Dancy,** Ph.D., is the third Helen S. Faison Endowed Chair and Director of the Center for Urban Education in the School of Education at the University of Pittsburgh. He was the past Associate Dean for Community Engagement and Academic Inclusion in the Jeannine Rainbolt College of Education at the University of Oklahoma. An education sociologist, Dancy studies educational settings as sites for social identity development. His research focuses on issues of access and equity in the educational pipeline as informed by race, gender, class, and other sociopolitical locations.

**Timothy DuWhite** is a black, queer, poz-writer/artist based out of Brooklyn, NY. A majority of his work circles around the intersections of state and body, state and love, and state and mind. All Timothy desires is a different/newer world for Black people, and believes the written word is one tool that could be used towards achieving that goal.

**Kirsten T. Edwards** is Linda Clarke Anderson Presidential Professor and Associate Department Chair of Educational Leadership & Policy Studies, as well as core affiliate faculty for African and African American Studies, Women's & Gender Studies, and the Center for Social Justice at the University of Oklahoma (OU) in Norman, Oklahoma. Her research merges philosophies of higher education, college curriculum, and pedagogy. More specifically, Dr. Edwards is interested in the ways that socio-cultural identity and context influence teaching and learning in post-secondary education.

**Jarvis R. Givens** is an assistant professor in the Harvard Graduate School of Education and the department of African and African American Studies at Harvard University. He is also the Suzanne Young Murray assistant professor at the Radcliffe Institute for Advanced Study. Givens' research focuses on the history of African American education in the 19th and 20th century, as well as critical theories of race, power, and schooling.

**Kevin Lawrence Henry, Jr.** is an assistant professor of Educational Policy Studies & Practice at the University of Arizona. His primary research and teaching focuses on the social contexts, political sociology, and cultural studies of education with an emphasis on racial capitalism, neoliberal restructuring, charter schools and school choice policy, and counter-hegemonic practices and theories.

**Tiffani Marie** is the daughter of Sheryll Marie and granddaughter of Dorothy and Annette. She has ancestral roots in Arkansas and Ghana and is a teacher and mentor to students in the H2O Program.

**Shameka N. Powell** is an assistant professor of Educational Studies in the Department of Education at Tufts University. Dr. Powell's research focuses on equality of opportunity and the intersections of race, class, gender in school spaces. They situate their research within Critical Race Theory and Queer of Color Theories.

**Shanara R. Reid-Brinkley** is co-director of Forensics and assistant professor of Race and Rhetoric in the Human Communication Studies Department at The California State University, Fullerton. She is the former Director of the William Pitt Debating Union and Assistant Professor of Public Address and Advocacy at the University of Pittsburgh. Dr. Reid-Brinkley is the 2018 Don Brownlee Award winner for Teaching, Scholarship and Service awarded by the Cross-Examination Debate Association.

**kihana miraya ross** is an assistant professor of African American Studies at Northwestern University. Her program of research examines the multiplicity of ways that antiblackness is lived by Black students and the ways Black educators and students engage in educational fugitivity to refuse and resist.

**David C. Turner III** is an activist scholar from Inglewood, California. His research focuses on youth-based social movements, political identity, and resistance to the prison regime. He currently works with boys and men of color organizations in Los Angeles County to end the school-to-prison pipeline and decriminalize communities of color.

**Hari Ziyad** is an artist, the author of *Black Boy Out of Time* (Little A, 2020) and the Editor-in-Chief of the digital publication *RaceBaitr*. They received their BFA from New York University, where they concentrated in Film and Television and Psychology. They are also the Managing Editor for *Black Youth Project* and an Assistant Editor for *Vinyl Poetry & Prose*.

# CONCEPT FIELD NOTES

## An Introduction

*Carl A. Grant*

## Third Week of April 2017

Authoring or editing a book materializes in its own unique way and with its own engaging story. Such is the case for *The Future is Black: Afropessism, Fugitivity and Radical Hope in Education*. For me, Carl, the seed for *The Future is Black* was planted during a lecture by Shanara Reid-Brinkley on Afropessimism. I do not recall hearing the term "afropessimism" before a student in my "Du Bois and Black Lives Matter" graduate class suggested that the class attend Reid-Brinkley's lecture, "Anti-Blackness and the Political: Millennials, Black Intellectuals, and the Re-shaping of American Politics." Attending the lecture sponsored by the Department of Sociology and the Haven's Center piqued my interest, for two reasons. One, here was an idea/concept (Afropessimism) that was garnering a great deal of attention from (young) Black scholars; and, two, the lecture convened an overflow crowd of predominately White graduate students in a very large room. The White audience of faculty and students, listened intently to Reed-Brinkley's comments on anti-blackness and the future of Black people. And, during the Q & A the mostly White audience remained sitting in quiet contemplation, or perplexity. Only a few, mostly clarifying, questions were raised. My scholarly curiosity, was thus, piqued, about "Afropessimism"—which reminded me of the work of Fanon and currently the writing of Ta-Nehisi Coates and other Black scholars, whose critical voices exhibit intellectual authority and responsibility in this puzzling time of ever-shifting and reinventing of race and racism; and my social/racial curiosity was raised by the "quiet contemplation and perplexity" of White folks. After the lecture, I introduced myself to Reid-Brinkley to tell her I have brought my *Du Bois* seminar to hear her and invited her to join us in an after-session in one of the empty classrooms. Accepting the invitation, Reid-Brinkley answered the questions my students eagerly asked and the students were delighted to have the opportunity to engage Reid-Brinkley directly on Afropessimism. That night, I read the several papers on Afropessimism that Reid-Brinkley had shared online.

The next afternoon, I took my undergraduate class of students who live together in the Multicultural Learning Community (MLC) to hear Reid-Brinkley's second lecture, "Black Radical Rhetoric(s): A Case Study in Black Youth Activism." Again, the large room was packed, and Reid-Brinkley's discussion of Afropessimism held the rapt attention of the audience, including the fifteen undergraduates from the MLC. In a debriefing session with the MLC students following the lecture, the students to a person were very pleased they had attended the lecture and during later meetings some students when discussing student activism referred back to her lecture.

## Fourth Week of April 2017

During the American Education Research Association (AERA) Annual Conference in San Antonio, Ashley Woodson and I had lunch together by chance. A crowed restaurant, my place at the front of a long line waiting for a table to eat, encouraged me to inviting Ashley and Kristen to join me for lunch. During lunch, with Afropessimism still buzzing in my head, I said, "Ashely what do you know about Afropessimism?" With that question, a flood gate of knowledge (definition, leaders in the field, debates, and papers to read) gushed forth from Ashely. "Wow!" was my response, followed momentarily by, "What are Black folks doing with this idea at AERA New York, in 2018?" When Ashley replied, "Nothing I know about," I replied, "Let's make something, happen!" My curiosity was heightened.

## First Week of May 2017

Returning to Madison, I began to think, "Here is an idea, a way of thinking, that seems mostly located in the disciplines of sociology and history, with some growing attention in education that could do with more visibility." Recently, completing a book with Kefferlyn and Anthony Brown, *Black Intellectual Thought in Education* (2015) and with my next book *Du Bois and Education* (2017), I am bluntly aware of the importance of Black intellectual thought and its need of visibility. Thus, I asked myself if it was possible to have an edited volume on Afropessimism and education for AERA, New York, 2018. I decided, "Why not?" And with that, I called Ashley and asked her if she would be interested in joining me on the project; and she immediately gave me a thumbs-up. However, when I ran the idea by Anthony (Brown) and Alex (Allweiss), they both asked me: "Why are you doing the book?", arguing Afropessimism wasn't my thing, and that I was invading the scholarly area of other scholars, especially Michael Dumas. Whereas that wasn't my intention at all, I did understand their reasoning and appreciated their observation. I then immediately called Michael, and to shorten this story, let me say he warmly agreed.

## Second Week in May – Second Week in October

The learning and collegial experience has been fabulous: ongoing conversations with Ashley and Michael, discussions with chapter authors and wonderful assistance from Routledge, especially Catherine Bernard.

Finally, as you read *The Future is Black: Afropessism, Fugitivity and Radical Hope in Education*, I am the protagonist for "radical hope," an idea that I contend is in the DNA of Black people and was observed during enslavement and continues to be observed today in spaces where Blacks are resisting and fighting back against various forms of cultural devastation. Enjoy the book, each chapter, including mine; it gives you thoughts to ponder.

THANKS, ASHLEY and MICHAEL.

# PART I
# Afropessimism and Fugitivity

# 1

# ON BLACK EDUCATION

## Anti-blackness, Refusal, and Resistance

*kihana miraya ross*

While I refuse to reproduce them here, we are tragically familiar with the plethora of anti-Black violence that makes the news—storylines often backed by video footage documenting Black children being terrorized or murdered. We also recognize that these bodies that are seen, these voices that are heard, are only a sliver of our reality—they do not represent the screams of the countless children whose stories remain untold. They do not (they cannot) fully articulate the stories of our babies, of the numerous Black children who grow up literally or metaphorically under the steel heel of a police boot. They do not exemplify the stories of the families, who for more than 400 years, have had to suffer the unimaginable losses of their children at the hands of state-sanctioned racialized terror.

And when parts of this terror flood our computer, phone, and television screens, these are just examples of experiences that may be more readily legible as anti-Black racism. These don't include the constant assaults levied against Black children and adults who are consistently found guilty of breathing while Black. News outlets and social media alike are flooded with daily accounts of Black people being harassed, assaulted, or even murdered for attempting to engage in mundane activities such as walking, standing, shopping, driving, playing, swimming, daring to wear our hair the way it naturally grows out of our heads and so forth. While hashtags such as #BBQBecky or #PermitPatty are ways of poking fun and pointing to the ridiculousness of the ways Black folks are consistently marked as other, these daily assaults contribute to the collective trauma of being racialized Black and having to navigate an anti-Black world.

While these examples are deliberately from out-of-school contexts, this is the society in which U.S. schools are created and maintained. These are the Black children who attend U.S. schools, and these are the Black families who rely on schools in this country to educate their children. Hence, in order to fully understand Black students' ongoing racialized experiences in schools, we have to understand the ways Black people, including children, are positioned in the larger world—the way blackness marks a particular ontological position. We have to interrogate the ways the Black body is read in a society whereby it was legitimately owned (juridically speaking); property to be bought and sold; used and abused as any white owner desired.

One way some Black scholars have articulated what it means to be marked as Black is through a theory of anti-blackness. While this terminology has become more readily used in recent years, both in academic circles and in the broader public, it is most often used to refer to racism against Black people. Yet, such an over-simplification effectively de-fangs this theoretical framework and erases its more complex ideas. Anti-blackness indexes the structural reality that in the larger society, blackness is inextricably tied to slaveness. While this doesn't mean that Black people are actually still enslaved by white slave masters, it does mean that slavery marks the ontological position of Black people—that the relation between humanity and blackness is an antagonism, is irreconcilable. This also necessitates shifting the normative center of gravity many scholars use when talking about racialized disparities—moving from white supremacy to anti-blackness, moving from white vs. non-white to Black vs. non-Black. Specifically, anti-blackness lays bare the problem with analogizing Black suffering to other forms of racialized suffering and argues that the differences are ontological rather than experiential. This way of conceptualizing anti-blackness comes out of what scholar Frank Wilderson (2010) came to call *Afro-pessimism*, a meta-theory that identifies this condition as permanent, one that will never be undone in this current world. Thus, if the relationship between blackness and humanity is a permanent antagonism, is irreconcilable, the goal of an Afro-pessimist project is to "destroy the world" (Wilderson, 2018). Wilderson's work is born out of a deep engagement with the work of other Black scholars such as Saidiya Hartman, Orlando Patterson, Hortense Spillers, and Sylvia Wynter.

One of the biggest elephants for someone trying to sit in an Afro-pessimist room is what this way of understanding the world says about resistance. If the project is about ending the world, what does that mean for what people actually do in the interim? Does Afro-pessimism reject the possibility of resistance in this world? There are two important points about resistance we find in Wilderson's writings (Wilderson, 2015, 2018). The first is what Wilderson often refers to as "setting it off." He uses this term to refer to those acts that throw a Molotov cocktail—literally or figuratively—into society in such a way that it disrupts, even for a moment, this world which bars Black access to humanity. Where the goal is the end of the world, any action that disrupts state-sanctioned anti-Black terror serves as a destruction teaser if you will, and Wilderson describes these acts as coming out of moments where we allow ourselves to sit with the impossibility of Black life. And the second point is just that—sitting with this impossibility. Wilderson's work suggests that if we can carve out space to sit with the reality—to move beyond calls to fix it, but rather to understand the fundamental antagonism and really stay there, that we will not muddy the waters with what are often non-Black imperatives toward solution—and we may find our way toward the beginning of the end.

In the education context, a small number of scholars have grown increasingly frustrated with what often feels like a circular conversation about the dissonance between what Black students may need from schools, and their actual anti-Black experiences. These scholars have looked to theoretical traditions in Black studies, namely Afro-pessimism, fugitivity, and abolition, to help make sense of an equation that never computes. Considering anti-blackness in education then, is about conceptualizing the experiences of Black students in schools through a different lens. Rather than dismissing work that, for example, interrogates the ways Black children are disproportionately referred out of the classroom, suspended, expelled, assaulted, arrested and so forth, we might ask ourselves what changes when we explore these racialized realities through the lens of anti-blackness in education? While it is necessary to interrogate the opportunity gap, underrepresentation of Black students in advanced courses, curricular misrepresentation and erasure, lack of access to quality teachers, counselors, material resources, and so forth, how might our understanding of these racialized disparities shift when we view them through the lens of anti-blackness? More broadly, what is the utility of a theory of anti-blackness in education? What are the possibilities it opens up? What tensions does it reveal? What might it foreclose?

This book is the first of its kind and attempts to wrestle with some of these challenging questions. Yet as the title of the book suggests, while anti-blackness in education may frame the conversation, the chapters herein also interrogate ideas of refusal, resistance, and what it means to maintain hope in schools and in a world structured by anti-Black solidarity (Wilderson, 2010). The book is divided into three parts: Afropessimism and Fugitivity, Conceptual Considerations, and Research Vignettes. In the first section, the authors consider the utility of working with theories of Afro-pessimism and fugitivity in the educational context. In order to ground the concept of fugitivity historically, Givens' chapter provides a robust theorization of fugitivity and reminds the reader that this is not just a word we may use to signal escape from educational suffering, but rather, it is tied to flesh and fear and tenacity of Black folks attempting to escape the suffocating dehumanization of chattel slavery. Givens writes,

> Scholars in Black Studies have borrowed the trope of fugitivity from the historicity of enslaved people resorting to various modes of escape— running away, hiding in the trunk of a tree, or the establishment of maroon societies in various African diasporic sites… Thus, fugitivity is forwarded as an analytic that extends from a precise temporal, historical reference. (p. 24)

Givens also makes plain that fugitivity is not a destination as "no practice of escape has been permanent for Black people" (p. 24). Givens' chapter suggests "the pursuit of education in service of transcending Black unfreedom has never successfully absolved that suffering but has more so been a meaningful way of existing in spite of it" (p. 24).

In my own work in this collection on *Black educational fugitive space*, I center the framework of fugitivity in part because in the educational context, the places that Black students and educators often utilize to produce Black space are tentative and can be taken away at any moment (Baldridge, 2019). They are usually set aside through a district initiative (i.e. Nasir et al., 2013) or at the individual school level (i.e ross, 2019), or part of the myriad after school and weekend programs that are supported through the non-profit sector. In each of these cases, a superintendent, principal, or executive director of a non-profit may change their minds or be replaced by someone who has a different vision. Districts, schools, and non-profits may lose funding and no longer be (willing or) able to support programming for Black students. So despite the ways Black students and educators resist anti-blackness through the production of Black space, this escape is not permanent but rather an interstitial space—a wading in the water with dreams of abolition.

Still, the production of Black educational fugitive space is a necessary weapon Black students may wield against their anti-Black experiences in schools. This is perhaps why Woodson's chapter suggests we should celebrate fugitivity and our status as fugitives. Woodson's chapter argues, "Black people are fugitives, not because we have escaped enslavement but because we have escaped the escape" (p. 19), and that "fugitive achievement is for the community" (p. 20). Hence for Woodson, fugitivity no longer signals escape but moves us beyond escape into a recognition that "we are already enough" (p. 19). Still, conceptualizing fugitivity in education may also require suggesting that fugitivity is not a celebratory "place" at which we have arrived, nor is it somewhere we may desire to stay. It is movement—continuous, unending, necessary, and oftentimes arduous movement because being on the move is the only way we can survive. In the educational context, it shapes our existence because in the *afterlife of school segregation* (see ross' chapter in this collection), the production of Black space will always be a fugitive endeavor. This does not discount the significance of envisioning otherwise possibilities (Nxumalo & ross, 2019), of engaging abolition imaginaries, or even of celebrating the genuine eye smiles and belly laughs shared in fugitive spaces. Rather, it is a reminder that fugitivity is not jubilee, but rather, a liminal existence between the "no longer and the not yet" (Best & Hartman, 2005, p. 3 as cited in Givens, this collection).

While the bulk of the chapters directly or indirectly focus on K-12 experiences, Dancy and Edwards' chapter highlights the need to move beyond the rhetoric of bias, diversity, and discrimination in higher education, and toward a more robust interrogation of anti-blackness and the ways "the degradation and denial of

Black life…is a necessary (re)articulation of enslavement" (p. 37). Dancy and Edwards argue that Black academics often endure the residue of colonial labor relations and have differentiated labor expectations. Their chapter questions the logical course forward if Black scholars engage an Afro-pessimist analysis and considers the possibilities in divestment, refusal, and abandonment. Ziyad and DuWhite's chapter also suggest a kind of divestment but from "gender disparity logic" that refuses to account for anti-blackness and thus perpetuates ongoing Black suffering. While the authors acknowledge that Black folks have experiences that are gendered in important ways, they argue,

> Black people's unique relationship to 'nothingness' as required by our lack of human subjecthood means that there is no matrix. Black suffering exists outside of the realm of human comparison, and therefore cannot be understood within a human hierarchy of violence, especially given the un-imaginability of Black childhood. (p. 158)

The authors argue for a refusal of hierarchical Black suffering matrices and a recognition that blackness has its own gendered integrity that can resist humanistic disparity logics that erase and criminalize Black children.

The second section of this book considers ideas of hope, resistance, and the intellectual connection between Afro-pessimism and racial realism. Grant forwards the idea of radical hope and considers what this concept means in the educational context. Grant conceptualizes radical hope in education as "hope that develops out of suffering and mourning, the destruction of a way life in the face of anxiety and uncertainty" (p. 66) and considers "the role of radical hope in the struggle for freedom and the acceptance and appreciation of Black humanity" (p. 67). While Grant takes seriously the realities of anti-blackness, this chapter cautions against the notion that Black folks' hope is false. Whereas Afro-pessimism does not believe in the possibility of a recognition of Black humanity in this current world, Grant argues it is precisely the radical hope Black folks have in education and in the future generations that "enables them to believe African Americans will continue to develop new narratives and traditions, and will come to see their humanity accepted and appreciated equal to any other humanity" (p. 70).

Brown and Brown's chapter focuses specifically on the ways anti-Black racism in school curriculum has historically been levied against Black children, and the ways it continues to function contemporarily. They suggest that part of the significance of school curriculum is that, "When this knowledge positions Blackness in an anti-Black fashion, it anchors in place for students, myopic meanings of Blackness and Black people" (p. 74). The authors argue anti-blackness in curriculum made Black folks into what Mills (1997) calls sub-person and perhaps what some education scholars have conceptualized as sub-students (Leonardo, 2013; ross et al, 2016). This rendering occurs through the utilization of the space of schools to proffer anti-Black ideas, through curriculum's ability to include or exclude stories of Black history and life, and through the ways anti-blackness in school curriculum has continued into the present (Brown & Brown 2010 as cited in Brown & Brown this collection). Brown and Brown also highlight the myriad ways folks have resisted anti-Black racism in school curriculum—both in the historical and contemporary context—and they end with a recognition of both the terror and hope of Black life in the U.S.

Henry and Powell work through the intellectual connection between Derrick Bell's racial realism and the way Afro-pessimism takes up Patterson's (1982) social death. The authors suggest that there is a bond between these two theoretical concepts which have both been critiqued for refusing a liberalist approach to Black freedom. Perhaps most importantly, the authors push the reader to consider how we forge a path forward. They argue:

> Racial realism and social death as constructs push us toward clarity regarding domination in the United States and provokes us to extinguish policy and pedagogic practices that reinscribe stratification and anti-Blackness. It pushes us to resist anti-Blackness and liberal fantasies. As such, educators and policymakers must grapple with the specific deep, everyday, normalized violence Black students, families, and educators face and continually work to dismantle it. Racial realism and social death frees us to imagine, hope, and build new futures rooted in Black liberation and freedom knowing that our survival, joy, and love requires us to, as Toni Morrison (1973) notes, "set about creating something else to be" (p. 52). (p. 84)

In a recent elaboration of BlackCrit (Dumas & ross, 2016; ross, 2019), I suggest that the utility in BlackCrit and really in considering Afro-pessimism in education more broadly, is about recognizing the ways anti-blackness functions in U.S. schools and that this condition is irreconcilable. I argue that in recognizing these schools as fundamentally irredeemable for Black children, that "they schools" (dead prez, 2000) will never be ours, we are better positioned to conceptualize liberatory educational possibilities for Black children. At the same time, I reiterate that this recognition does not mean that we simply give up on schools and do nothing—quite the contrary, as Black children will likely remain in these institutions for decades to come. This necessitates us giving attention to what I call the "meantime in between time," or what it is that we can do right now to mitigate Black suffering in schools and make the educational experiences of Black students better. The final section of the book, Research Vignettes, considers how we may think through and with theories of anti-blackness, fugitivity, and radical hope in education in our empirical work, and in our collective and ongoing efforts to "do something" now for Black children in U.S. public schools.

While this book is organized into three distinct sections, certainly all of the sections are interrogating what it means to both acknowledge the myriad ways Black students navigate the afterlives of slavery (Hartman, 1997, 2007), and also, the ways they refuse, resist, and reimagine. These final chapters center empirical work with Black youth and encourage us to think deeply about what it means to re(view) this work through a lens of anti-blackness. Carey's chapter for example, interrogates how Black boys may resist in the wake, in part, through imagining otherwise possibilities. Like Grant's chapter on radical hope, Carey also ruminates on the ways the future life Samuel (the boy in his study) imagines, signals a radical hope—that "simply imagining a future that is so divergent from anything in close proximity to Black boys in urban settings is a radical act" (p. 92). Carey suggests that the project of Afro-pessimism is to engage Afro-futurities, and that one duty of educators of Black children is to guide Black students through future-oriented learning experiences to resist the ways their futures are un-imagined. Marie's chapter also considers what it means for Black boys to navigate anti-blackness in schools and resist the hopelessness their worlds may attempt to impose.

The penultimate two chapters consider the radical possibilities of an Afro-pessimist lens for engaging in social activism for youth and adults. Reid-Brinkley's chapter cautions against the notion that engaging young people in the realities of anti-blackness necessitates robbing them of potential or actual hope. As opposed to destroying "the beauty of youthful hope" (p. 101), Afro-pessimism can "galvanize a different kind of hope that is generative and sustaining toward dreaming of new futures" (p. 101). Reid-Brinkley suggests Black debaters are "developing rhetorical and argumentative strategies to engage anti-blackness and build new relationships to futurity" (p. 101). Turner's chapter also considers the utility of Afro-pessimism in engaging young people in social activism. However, Turner would argue that anti-Black realities necessarily diminish Black organizers' abilities to encourage hope. He writes, "Even though our jobs are to inspire hope, the condition of Blackness does not allow hopes to get too high" (p. 112). Turner reminds us that Black liberation may require uncivil resistance, and suggests that the job of Black organizers is to facilitate the kind of political consciousness that will lead to uncivility. In his words, "Organizing for (un)civility means being a bad citizen. It means breaking rules. It means not consenting to the demands placed on you by white civil society to make things happen" (p. 113) and "what we need to be organizing for is chaos" (p. 114).

In the current Black educational landscape, an increasing number of scholars are looking to theoretical traditions in Black studies to consider what anti-blackness and anti-Black racism in the larger society mean for the education of Black children in the U.S. Here I want to return to questions posed earlier: What is the utility of a theory of anti-blackness in education? What are the possibilities it opens up? What tensions does it reveal? What might it foreclose?

I want to suggest that the utility in thinking through and with theories of anti-blackness and anti-Black racism in education is about recognizing the ways anti-blackness functions in U.S. schools, and ultimately clarifying the fundamental incompatibility of Black liberation and public schooling in these United States. In other words, where Afro-pessimism very clearly articulates the idea that blackness is coterminous with slaveness, education scholars may draw on this theory to explicate the ways Black students are positioned as substudents, marked as inherently uneducable. Where Afro-pessimism argues that the relationship between blackness and humanity is an antagonism, is irreconcilable, education scholars may consider the ways the relationship between Black students and the structure of U.S. schooling is irreconcilable. The notion of the afterlife of school segregation is about a specificity of experience—about refusing linear narratives of black educational progress that fail to align with the lived experiences of black students—about being precise in our interrogations of the myriad ways Black students in particular continue to live in the afterlife of slavery. It is also about rendering the quotidian assaults on Black students legible as part and parcel of the ways schools remain structured by anti-Black solidarity.

Finally, as we continue to grapple with anti-blackness and anti-Black racism in education, we must contend with what different Black folks want for their children and what that means for the ways our emancipatory visions take shape. As we theorize both Black educational realities and futurities and possibilities, we must remember we are talking about our babies. Certainly this isn't to insinuate that we have to have solutions to unearth or elaborate a problem. We don't. Rather, we should ensure that as we continue to dream, we are dreaming together. That we are building with Black parents, teachers, students, activists, and communities more broadly, to both speak the truth of our realities and also, to chart our path forward. That we are always talking to folks racialized Black in this world to continue to ensure our ideas reflect actual experiences and desires, and that our imaginings are part of the ongoing collective struggle for Black life and living.

## References

Baldridge, B. J. (2019). *Reclaiming Community: Race and the Uncertain Future of Youth Work*. Standford, CA: Stanford University Press.

Dead Prez (2000). They Schools on *Let's Get Free* [Vinyl, LP, Album]. New York, NY: Loud Records.

Dumas, M. J., & ross, k. m. (2016). "Be real Black for me": Imagining BlackCrit in education. *Urban Education, 51*(4), 415–442.

Hartman, S. (1997). *Scenes of Subjection*. New York: Oxford University Press.

Hartman, S. V. (2007). *Lose Your Mother: A Journey Along the Atlantic Slave Route*. New York, NY: Farrar, Straus and Giroux.

Nasir, N. ross, k. m., Mckinney de Royston, M., Givens, J., & Bryant, J. (2013). Dirt on my record: Rethinking disciplinary practices in an all-Black, all-male alternative class. *Harvard Educational Review, 83*(3), 489–512.

Nxumalo, F., & ross, k. m. (2019). Envisioning Black space in environmental education for young children. *Race Ethnicity and Education, 22*(4), 502–524.

ross, k.m. (2018). Ties that bind: Forging Black girl space in the Black (male) educational "crisis". In Nasir, N., Givens, J., & Chatmon, C. (Eds.), *We Dare Say Love: Supporting African American Male Achievement.* New York, NY: Teachers College Press, Multicultural Education Series.

ross, k.m. (2019). *Revisiting BlackCrit in Education: Anti-Black Reality and Liberatory Fantasy.* CCRSE Research Brief, no. 17. Los Angeles, CA: Center for Critical Race Studies at UCLA.

ross, k.m., Nasir, N., Givens, J., McKinney de Royston, M, Vakil, S., Madkins, T., & Philoxene, D. (2016). "I do this for all of the reasons America doesn't want me to": The organic pedagogies of Black male instructors. *Equity & Excellence in Education, 49*(1), 85–99.

Wilderson III, F. B. (2010). *Red, White & Black: Cinema and the Structure of U.S. Antagonisms.* Durham, NC: Duke University Press.

Wilderson, F. B. (2015). *Afro-pessimism and the End of Redemption.* Retrieved from https://humanitiesfutures.org/papers/afropessimism-end-redemption/

Wilderson, F. B. (2018). "We're trying to destroy the world": Anti-blackness and police violence after Ferguson. In *Shifting Corporealities in Contemporary Performance* (pp. 45–59). Cham: Palgrave Macmillan.

# 2

# AFROPESSIMISM FOR US IN EDUCATION

## In Fugitivity, through Fuckery and with Funk

*Ashley N. Woodson*

Many of the mainstream Black social reform movements that followed the Emancipation Proclamation have demanded access to equitable public schooling in some capacity. In the years leading up to the 1954 Brown v. Board of Education decision, these demands often included separate but equal school facilities. Black activists who supported the separate but equal doctrine wanted buildings, textbooks and technology that were of the same nature and quality as those found in middle-class white districts.

The popularity of separate but equal as both a legal and social philosophy in Black communities should not be understated. There were a number of Black folks, including many Southern Black teachers, who felt that school desegregation would prove harmful to Black children. These folks worried that desegregation would undermine the cultural leadership of Negro teachers, eliminate positions for Negro teachers and principals and deter Negro students from becoming teachers. They expressed concern that white teachers would not understand Negro children. Further, they argued that school desegregation would discourage racial pride and curtail the self-expression of Negro children. "Negroes," according to one summary of this position, "do not want to be where they are merely tolerated."

The Black architects of the Brown v. Board prosecution framed the potential of school desegregation differently. They chose to argue against the separate but equal doctrine, insisting instead that the harms of racial isolation outweighed the benefits of maintaining de jure segregated Black school districts. Attorney and eventual Supreme Court Justice Thurgood Marshall was the National Association for the Advancement of Colored People Chief Council for Brown v. Board of Education. He argued that segregated schools were:

> of major concern to the individual of public school age and contributes greatly to the unwholesomeness and unhappy development of the

personality of Negroes which the color caste system in the United States has produced.

Ultimately, the Supreme Court would rule in favor of Marshall and the NAACP attorneys throughout Delaware, South Carolina, Virginia, Kansas and the District of Columbia who championed racial desegregation in public schools. In the Brown majority opinion, the Court held that racial segregation "generates a feeling of inferiority ... that may affect [Black children's] hearts and minds in a way unlikely ever to be undone."

After the Brown majority opinion, public schools in the United States were to be desegregated with "all deliberate speed." Spoiler alert: *all deliberate speed* meant really, really, really slow. All deliberate speed was standard English for a lackadaisical, pendulous pace that (as of this writing) spans the better part of a century. The frustrating truth is, we may never know which perspectives on the separate but equal doctrine most closely aligned with the best educational interests of Black people. The partial implementations of school desegregation that have emerged are certainly not representative of Justice Marshall's vision. The social mobility bag has been secured for some Black people in some desegregated settings. But the human and professional toll prophesied by early 20th-century Southern Black teachers has devastated the Black educational infrastructure. If one thousand modern Black people were transported to testify during the Brown hearings, there would probably be one thousand unique, reflective and trauma-informed stories about the consequences of school desegregation.

It is the trauma in those stories that motivates much of the critical inquiry into the possibilities for Black kids in public schools. The conditions of pre-Brown school segregation probably did contribute to a robust and painful awareness of Black people's structural inferiority in the United States. But we can't honestly argue that post-Brown learning conditions have ameliorated Black subordination in any meaningful way. The traumas of desegregation are found in the number of displaced Black teachers, school closures and school takeovers in Black communities. Trauma is inflicted by racialized disparities in sense of belonging, standardized test scores, and patterns of discipline. Trauma is measured in the minutes of lost sleep as Black children wake up for an earlier bus, the gas to a parent teacher conference across the city, or the number of pages a student flips through before they see their interests represented in a textbook.

For many, trauma is now apparent in the historical insistence that Black children's wholeness was only accessible through the forms of schooling designed to serve middle-class white children and sustain white supremacy.

Critical inquiry into this trauma has been guided by multiple overlapping frameworks. This text introduces Afropessimism, a series of claims about the Black diasporic condition that center the *maafa* – a Swahili term that references the chaos, disaster and tragedy of the Transatlantic Slave Trade and its aftermath – as the essential climacteric in understanding the possible futures of African and African descended people. A core premise is that slavery, colonialism and apartheid have permanently altered the material, cultural and spiritual lives of Black people, and thus, the material, cultural and spiritual lives of everyone who inhabits the world with Black people. Coordinated global campaigns to theologically, politically, legally and economically rationalize Black people as property mark a moral point of no return.

But be careful as you wade into the archives, family. We are careful because the language of Afropessimism has been around since at least the 1980s. The term is invoked to represent two distinct and irreconcilable collections of ideas. I call the first collection of ideas "vulgar Afropessimism." It mostly consists of white supremacist musings and half-baked rationales for settler colonialism. The second collection of ideas is "critical Afropessimism." This more contemporary intellectual movement engages theories of Black liberation, and informs the writings in this volume.

Afropessimism was originally used to describe worldviews wherein Black Africans lacked the moral, political or economic aptitude to dismantle postcolonial corruption. This vein of thinking is an echo of Hegel's 19th century argument that the continent called Africa represented no cultural "movement or development." Drawing on records of European missionaries (colonizers with Bibles), explorers (colonizers with maps) and pseudo-scientists (colonizers with lab coats), Hegel contended that the stories of Africans should not register within the annals of human history. Africa was a series of godless, hedonistic and savage accidents. The continent and its diverse people were doomed to remain "wild," "untamed," and "undeveloped."

Fast forward to the early nineties, when Hegel's vision of Africa is very much alive in Fukuyama's *The End of History and the Last Man*. Fukuyama argued that Western liberal democracies were the penultimate benchmark of human achievement. He discredited the models of self-determination that preceded and sustain African communities (in favor of the models of government that have *obviously* eliminated social inequity and violence in the West). Fukuyama is not referenced to suggest a renaissance of vulgar Afropessimism in the 1990s, this way of thinking remained prevalent in Judeo-Christian theology, international policy and popular culture. Michael Jackson's entire 1985 We Are the World: USA for Africa music video and campaign. The May 2000 cover of *The Economist* depicting an African man holding a missile gun under the heading "The hopeless continent." The photo of a beautiful, skeptical and unnamed Black boy whose presumed suffering animates a viral meme. Vulgar Afropessimism cites the civil wars and political turmoil that often accompany Western colonial intrusion as evidence that Africa simply can't keep up without Western inspiration and support.

At the turn of the 21st century, the language of Afropessimism was reappropriated to label something like a countermovement. Many of those who named the movement were Black folks trained and employed in Western institutions, with notable advancements in the fields of cultural studies, literary theory and philosophy. On at least one point, the critical Afropessimists agree with the vulgar Afropessimists: Black people are totally fucked. Critical Afropessimists do not believe that African and African descended people are not doomed because they lack certain aptitudes. Instead, continued Black despair results from the extent to which Black communities and Blackness are regarded as illegitimate points of reference for understanding the human experience.

In other words, this fuckery is not our fault. We (and by we I mean us) will also never be free of this fuckery, because there is no authority to petition for our freedom. Global systems of governance were created to manage our enslavement and exploitation, and the pillars of those systems organize the expansion of empire still today. Nearly every social institution in the United States is fashioned to accommodate and preserve our subordination, or to otherwise compromise the humanity of Black people, including schools. Here is where critical Afropessimism informs historical and contemporary debates about the school desegregation, and questions about separate but equal philosophies. In a humble but confident critique of our foreparents, critical Afropessimists question the necessity and pursuit of *equal*.

Black equality is an ontological impossibility. It is an inappropriate benchmark that ties our pursuit of recognition to capitalism, privatization and ownership. This is not a particularly innovative claim, as it echoes previous contentions by Frantz Fanon, Claudia Jones and Derrick Bell. Critical Afropessimism situates this claim within an expanded context, with an emerging awareness of past failures and past potentials. (That's all critical ever means, really, that time has offered insights that our ancestors did not have.) Critical Afropessimism depicts a world in which schools are established sites of immense social suffering and estrangement for Black children. In this world, the idea of *equal* is so maliciously compelling that Black caregivers, teachers, activists and scholars misrepresent the interests of all of our children so that a few might fall beneath the shadow of *equal*'s promise. We teach our babies to pursue *equal* status with those whose (access to) life is defined by our (vulnerability to) death.

Black humanity is an ontological reality. We are already enough. With no further recognition, we are already enough. With no new legislation, we are already enough. If there is never another Black first or Black millionaire or Black prodigy. We. Are. Already. Enough. Already. In critical veins of Afropessimism, this mantra is described as Black fugitivity. Black people are fugitives, not because we have escaped enslavement but because we have escaped the escape. We do not run anymore, family. We take root in our enoughness and laugh at the arbitrariness of our exclusion. If you desire firstness, then firstness is for you. But you were enough before it. If you desire millions, do no harm to your own in your pursuit of it. You were enough when you were broke.

Engineer, dance, formulate, sing, create, run, write. Do you. Do us. And celebrate. Like a fucking fugitive.

Fugitive achievement is for the community, but not on behalf of the community. No Black person is a representative for Black communities to a presumed arbitrator of our worth. As already enoughs, celebration of achievement does not require invocation of our previous pursuit of *equal*. Our celebrations are rejections of that premise, or they are not celebrations at all. Celebrate enoughness. Celebrate the child who cared for siblings as often as you celebrate the child with perfect attendance. The children who queer your understanding of beauty and the children clothed in glory at prom. The rape survivor and the star athlete. The child who never shot at the innocent and the child with perfect attendance. All of these children are enough. Insist on our enoughness.

Insist on celebration. I celebrate you, still reading, because there is one who stopped reading 387 words ago. Though some will disagree, I believe that fugitive achievement and celebratory acts are the core of critical Afropessimist practice. Moten described celebration as the essence of Black thought. Black thought and celebration are inextricably linked, because our thinking is our movement toward sustained fugitivity. Moten added, "the cause for celebration turns out to be the condition of possibility ... which animates the black operations that will produce the absolute overturning, the absolute turning of this motherfucker out."

It is bad form to define a new concept in the concluding paragraph of an essay. I apologize family, but complicated jargon like *turn this motherfucker out* necessitates clarity and precision. For this review I derive methodologies for *turning this motherfucker out* primarily from two theorists in addition the above cited Moten. First, Smitherman's use of "turn it out" is pivotal. Operationalizing the phrasing within epistemologies of Black language traditions, she defined the concept in this way:

> To create a scene, causing people to vacate a place. 2) To party aggressively, loudly and with wild abandon, partying until the place is emptied out.

Second, funk music collective Parliament-Funkadelic suggested that we *turn this mother out* in pursuit of what we want, need and gotta have. In their groundbreaking work "Tear the Roof off the Sucker," the collective posits that what we want, need and gotta have is the funk. Parliament-Funkadelic founder George Clinton defined funk as "anything you need it to be to save your life."

We can turn this desegregation thing out. This does not mean in every instance that we walk away from what we have built, what we have earned, or what we are owed. Some might, some can. But as we engage critical Afropessimism and its possibilities, we must remember that it is impractical to advocate for forms of fugitivity that only get some of us together. Desegregation structures the lives and aspirations of many Black folk, and we should not be so woke that we are asleep to these realities. Turning desegregation out means rejecting the assumption that being merely tolerated through desegregation makes us more enough. It is aggressively celebrating with and for Black children until this assumption is vacated and condemned.

## Works Cited

Brown v. Board of Education, 347 U.S. 483 (1954).

Clinton, G. (2015). George Clinton Lecture at the Red Bull Music Academy, New York. Retrieved from: https://www.youtube.com/watch?v=A7MlcvfcGW8/.

Dumas, M. J. (2014). "Losing an arm": schooling as a site of black suffering. *Race Ethnicity and Education, 17*(1), 1–29.

Fukuyama, F. (2006). *The end of history and the last man.* Simon & Schuster.

Gumbs, A. P. (2016). *Spill: Scenes of black feminist fugitivity.* Duke University Press.

Marshall, T. (2003). *Supreme justice: Speeches and writings.* University of Pennsylvania Press.

Moten, F. (2013). Blackness and nothingness (mysticism in the flesh). *South Atlantic Quarterly, 112*(4), 737–780.

Rosenthal, J. O. (1957). Negro teachers' attitudes toward desegregation. *The Journal of Negro Education, 26*(1), 63–71.

Smitherman, G. (2000). *Black talk: Words and phrases from the hood to the amen corner.* Houghton Mifflin Harcourt.

Verharen, C. C. (1997). "The New World and the dreams to which it may give rise." An African and American response to Hegel's challenge. *Journal of Black Studies, 27*(4), 456–493.

# 3

# LITERATE SLAVE, FUGITIVE SLAVE

## A Note on the Ethical Dilemma of Black Education

*Jarvis R. Givens*

The below passage is taken from Katherine McKissack's historical-fiction novel for children, entitled *A Picture of Freedom*. This story of Clotee, an enslaved girl in Virginia, was inspired by accounts of McKissack's "great-great-great grand-mother who dared to learn and teach." But Clotee's story entails a striking res-onance with Frederick Douglass' iconic narrative of fugitive literacy, and many other lesser known stories, such as Jenny Procter of Alabama, an enslaved woman born in 1850 (Douglass, 1855, p. 155; Proctor & Federal Writers Project, 1937). Procter recalled that she was not "lowed to see a book or try to learn." Despite these restrictions, she employed transgressive tactics to learn anyhow. "We slips around and gits hold of that Webster's old blue-back speller and we hides til 'way in the night and then we lights a little pine torch, and we studies the spelling book" (Proctor & Federal Writers Project, 1937, p. 2). In her fictional account, McKissack writes the following from the perspective of Clotee:

> As long as it's hot I have to fan young Mas' William and Miz Lilly, my mistress, during their study time. This mornin' was the first day of my third learnin' season. For now on three years, I been fannin' them, liftin' and lowerin' the big fan made of woven Carolina sweet grass—up and down, up and down. The fan stirs the thick air ... and chases away wor-risome horse flies and eye gnats. It may seem like a silly job. But, I don't mind one bit, 'cause while William is learnin', so am I ... I got to be real particular and make sure nobody finds out though, 'cause if my mas'er finds out I would fall under the whip. (McKissack, 1997, pp. 3–4)

Clotee, along with Douglass and Proctor, represents a heritage of "*learn-ing as a means of escape* [italics added]," as the famed educator and historian

Carter G. Woodson phrased it (Woodson, 1922, p. 108). Her disavowing of the moral standards that forbade literacy because of her status as a marked woman underscores a critical gesture in the heritage of Black education. In this essay, I assert that the enslaved person stealing away to gain literacy represents the quintessential persona (and political tension) at the heart of Black education, a project that dwells on the question of freedom and has historically required a fugitive disposition toward dominant schooling norms.

Our gaze toward Black education is always routed through the memory of slavery and Black people's violent exclusion from the American schooling project, and rightfully so. It signals the terms of relation between Black learners and institutions of schooling. What's more, as the project of Black education formally developed, it continued to be riddled by an inherent ethical dilemma— precisely that any purposeful education for Black people continued to require subversive approaches in both content and process (Givens, 2016; Siddle Walker, 1996; Watkins, 1993; Webber, 1978). This is a part of a critical Black educational memory (or heritage), whereby we recall our history of contingent citizenship and how it has always mirrored our relationship to the American school, and vice versa. This context prompts the question at the core of this chapter: what does it mean for Black education to be in service to freedom dreams within the American schooling project, a project that is inherently anti-Black?

From its inception, Black education was always already in ethical crisis. To insist on Black rationality was to contest the Western world's sentient and epistemological assertion that Blacks were ineducable, or to some degree rationally incapacitated (Givens, 2016; Thomas, 2006). It was an insisting on Black humanity within a national body politic (and world structure) that deemed Black people to be beneath the threshold of human history and development. This antagonism was/is at the heart of the matter. What Clotee and Proctor signal for us today is a lesson of what it means to exist with an inner divergence as Black learners, to hold oneself apart from the circumstances of anti-Black structures of education even as we wade through it. This is the ethical dilemma at the core of Black educational life—its demanding of "fugitive spirit," in the mind and flesh (Mackey, 1992, p. 55).

This chapter sets out to accomplish three things: first, to conceptualize the meaning of fugitivity as an analytic with a utilitarian bearing on how we might interpret Black education as a historical, political endeavor; second, to speak pointedly about the ways in which Black teachers (and students) have necessarily inhabited a fugitive stance within the American school; and third, to discuss what this historicity of Black fugitivity in education means for our 21st century present.

## Black Education as a Fugitive Project

By the time emancipation was granted in 1865, the issuing of the 13th Amendment, or the establishment of Freedmen's schools, it had already happened.

Black education had taken root as a fugitive project. It was mobilized as an activity of escape, violating the parameters of Black Americans' curtailed citizenship and position as legally *and then* civically unfree.

Scholars in Black Studies have borrowed the trope of fugitivity from the historicity of enslaved people resorting to various modes of escape—running away, hiding in the trunk of a tree, or the establishment of maroon societies in various African diasporic sites. Not to mention its harkening to the Fugitive Slave Act of 1850, which deputized slave catchers to seek and return Blacks *accused* of running away, even if they were settled in states where slavery was abolished. Building on the work of Black literary scholars and cultural theorists, James Edward Ford III defined fugitivity as "a critical category for examining *the artful escape of objectification*, whether said objectification occurs through racialized aesthetic framing, commodification, or liberal juridico-political discourse" (Ford, 2014, p. 3). Thus, fugitivity is forwarded as analytic that extends from a precise temporal, historical reference. The analytic denotes escape in both a physical and psychic sense (Roberts, 2015). On another note, the liminality of the fugitive slave is particularly important when thinking through this analytic, a distinction that becomes clear when interrogating the limitations of escape or, more precisely, the lurking possibility of recapture. Recall here Clotee's evocation of "the whip"—if her literacy is *found* out.

### The Threat of Recapture and the Limits of Escape

Even as the captive has escaped from bondage, the contingencies of their escape and the looming threat of recapture signals their liminality—a phenomenological in-betweenness—escape's lack of definitiveness. To this point, Stephen Best and Saidiya Hartman wrote the following regarding fugitivity: it is "the political interval in which all captives find themselves—the interval between the no longer and the not yet, between the destruction of the old world and the awaited hour of deliverance … this is the master-trope of Black political discourse. In this interval we find the mutual imbrication of pragmatic political advance with a long history of failure" (Best & Hartman, 2005, p. 3). Thus, while the fugitive slave is no longer in physical bondage, they are yet not free. Fugitivity denotes a particular set of contingencies of Black political and social life during slavery and post-emancipation, as Black American's existed within the vestibule of freedom and citizenship.

What is revealed here, with unrelenting clarity, is that no practice of escape has been permanent for Black people. As it follows, the pursuit of education in service of transcending Black unfreedom has never successfully absolved that suffering but has more so been a meaningful way of existing in spite of it. To this point, Fred Moten aptly notes (and I paraphrase)—escape is an activity, it's not an achievement (John Hope Franklin Humanities Institute, 2016).

## Black Exclusion from the Common School and the Development of Fugitive Demands

The fugitive spirit in Black education took distinguishable form during the early 19th century, alongside, and in tandem with, the development of the Common School Movement. In my other work, I argue that the competing discourses of the Common School Movement, abolitionism, and anti–Black educational policies (such as anti–Literacy laws) converged and informed a shared ethic/rationale amongst Black Americans that education and freedom were inextricably bound. The Common School Movement, which gained notable traction in the 1830s, was explicit in its exclusion of Blacks from its program that ushered (white) youth into their rightful inheritance of national citizenship (Moss, 2009; Tyack, 1974). There was simultaneously the enactment of new laws and public discourse that made it illegal for enslaved and free Blacks to read and write across the South (Williams, 2007, pp. 203–14). Blacks had provisional (often separate) access to education in the North, but their experiences were undoubtedly shaped by anti-Blackness (Douglas, 2005). There was an increase of subversive educational acts on the parts of free and enslaved Blacks during these years.

African Americans took extreme measures to become educated during this time—literate Blacks started schools in secrecy across the South, some climbed into holes in the woods to attend school, literary societies developed among Northern Blacks as early as the 1820s and 1830s, and some even attempted to start a Black college as early as 1831 in New Haven—an effort that prompted outrage and protest amongst Yale students and professors who deemed it "unwarranted and dangerous" (Anderson, 1988; Douglas, 2005, p. 41; Porter, 1936; Williams, 2007, p. 5). In 1829, the radical Black abolitionist David Walker articulated a direct relationship between Black educational obtainment and his vision for a radical rebellion against slavery and Black oppression (Walker, 1830, p. 37). These historical events gesture towards the political ethos that undergirded the heritage being formed in Black educational life.

## Black Education was a Fugitive Project from its Inception

Frederick Douglass identified this political idea in his 1855 autobiography, when he declared, "knowledge unfits a child to be a slave." He came to this conclusion after the following proclamations uttered by Master Auld:

> Learning would spoil the best nigger in the world; if you teach that nigger—speaking of myself—how to read the bible, there will be no keeping him; it would forever unfit him for the duties of a slave … making him disconsolate and unhappy. If you learn him now to read, he'll want to know how to write; and, this accomplished, he'll be running away with himself. (Douglass, 1855, p. 146)

Hence, the literate slave evokes a slave running away—or worse, a slave "want[ing] to be a Nat Turner" (Douglass, 1855, p. 200). The terms of relation that characterize Black schooling took shape within this educational landscape, where the malignant sentiments of slavery shaped moral doctrines of literacy and the American schooling project. This discursive terrain engendered a counter-ideology that Black Americans would continue to build on as their access to schooling opportunities and positionality within the civic structure of America evolved. Black education persisted as an activity of escape—the material and socio-political realities of Black life demanded it as such.

## A Lesson from Jim Crow Teachers

As Black education developed from emancipation to Jim Crow, African American teachers often discerned an incongruence between their vested interests in education as a freedom-seeking project and their political and economic realities within the American educational landscape (Anderson, 1988; Fultz, 1995; Givens, 2016). Coming to this juncture, I want to suggest that there continues to be an under-theorization of Black teachers' pedagogies, their ideological orientations to educating Black students, and especially what happened (in a quotidian since) in the private spaces of their classrooms. In clarifying the subversive demands of Black education and the liminal space Black teachers were relegated to, we gain more nuance regarding their interior lives as stokers of Black freedom dreams, even while operating in the confinement of the American school.

The prevailing narrative of Black teachers has been confounded by a preoccupation with the politics of respectability, in which they embodied dominant conservative beliefs that enforced piety, temperance and cleanliness as an effort to disprove myths about Blacks as inferior and unworthy of equality. The "politics of respectability" was initially theorized by Evelyn Brooks Higginbotham (1994) to describe how Victorian standards of womanhood were used to police Black women's social and behavioral practices in an effort to demonstrate their civility to white society. The politics of respectability had implications across gendered boundaries, however; it required "that every individual in the Black community assume responsibility for behavioral self-regulation and self-improvement along moral, educational, and economic lines" (Higginbotham, 1994, p. 196).

### On Respectability and Fugitive Spirit

Black teachers often wore a mask of compliance and respectability even as they continued to embody a politicized pedagogy of resistance (Burkholder, 2012; Gilmore, 1996). An analysis that holds these politics in tension with one another offers a more productive optic. It illustrates how the fugitive project of Black education came to bear on their inner divergence from the oppressive structures teachers worked within. The current under-theorization belittles, for instance, Black teachers' cryptic and silent partnerships with the NAACP, which they intentionally kept hidden for reasons of job security (Siddle Walker, 2018). We might also recall Septima Clark's pedagogy premised on civic education, even as Southern Blacks were violently excluded from the civic structures of America and blocked from voting. Clark's pedagogy was shaped by an imagination of a world that had yet to exist, one based on a radical notion of equality, a world she was committed to forging (Charron, 2012). These examples denote Black educators "fugitive pedagogy" during the Jim Crow period.

In my other work I have discussed Black schoolteachers representation of Black achievement and slave insurrections in textbooks they published as early as 1890 (Givens, 2016). They wrote about figures like Phillis Wheatley and slave insurrectionists as "a living, breathing, convincing argument against the claim that the Negro's intellectual capacities fit him only for slavery" (Johnson, 1890, p. 84). While Black teachers may have been coerced into procedural compliance to Jim Crow schooling structures by a host of disciplinary technologies, these teachers often maintained a conceptual divergence from these structures; a divergence that shaped their orientation to teaching and caring for Black learners.

The disjuncture between performances of compliance and the fugitive planning of Black educators extends from the moral crisis inherent in the project of Black education. The incongruence between the overarching educational landscape and the moral commitments of Black teachers relegated them to a fugitive liminality—constantly stealing away to modes of escape, in one way or another. These teachers modeled what it looks and feels like to use the needs of Black learners as a compass toward a purposeful education, even within a schooling structure that was hostile to their very existence. They modeled what it means to be within, yet against the American school.

## So Now What?—What Does Fugitive Pedagogy Offer Us Today?

I hope to have made clear two foundational assertions. First, Black education emerged as a fugitive project by the early 19th century in response to the racial provisions of American common schooling and anti-Black educational policies (i.e. anti-literacy laws). Second, even as Black education became formalized, Black teachers continued to embody the ethical crisis of its origins. They were coerced to perform deference to the moral conventions of Jim Crow schooling, even as they embodied and taught fierce critiques of white supremacy beyond the eye of Jim Crow authorities.

Conversely, there are real limitations that we must contend with. When we envision the fugitive planning of Black teachers and the NAACP, or their textbooks that boldly held up rebellious Black historical figures, we must be careful not to give in so easily to the appeals for jubilee. Fugitivity is not a theory of resolution, but a descriptor of a core conflict in Black educational life and a particular posturing, or mode of being. School structures still had the power to punish Black teachers like Septima Clark, who was fired because of her involvement with the NAACP (recapture). Black teachers' textbooks rarely replaced the formerly adopted racist curricula. This is a reality of the relations of power, despite the infinite acts of subversion Black people engaged in over generations. What we see is the proliferation of "their straining against constraint" (Moten, 2007, p. 4). This is what became required of teachers and students to appropriate structures of learning for the daunting project of Black freedom.

This historical inventory of Black fugitive life in education offers some meditation on what is possible of Black subjectivity (being and becoming) within the confinement of anti-Black educational structures and as necessary criticism: fugitive spirit as a modality of teaching, learning and existing. This is not a rejection of learning and schooling, but an "inner divergence" and vigilance of school content and structures (Mackey, 1992, p. 54). While this assertion might seem pessimistic—a constant looking over one's shoulder—this appears to be the only means for Black social life to exist in schools; the alternatives are bleak. In turning towards the history of Black education—and not just formal institutional histories, but to the gaze of Black learners from outside the doors of the common school—I hope to have underscored the ethical dilemma we must confront. Any purposeful education (meaning an education in service to Black liberation) requires a steady practice of escape.

To be clear, this is not to suggest that all acquisition of education and academic achievement should be read as escape. Certainly Black educational attainment can be (and at times has been) overdetermined by acquiescence (Woodson, 2008; Zimmerman, 2010). The highest calling of Black education, however, has been its critical nature; its rootedness in/reflexivity of the space of marginality Black people are relegated to. In this tradition, Black education has functioned on a shadow curriculum that runs parallel to and as critique of dominant education (its imperialistic aims, assertions of knowledge, and technologies of stratification). It must necessarily be a shadow education, lest we run the risk of becoming that which required our exclusion to begin with.

## Works Cited

Anderson, J. (1988). *The Education of Blacks in the South, 1860–1935*. Chapel Hill: The University of North Carolina Press.

Best, S., & Hartman, S. (2005). Fugitive Justice. *Representations, 92*(1), 1–15. https://doi.org/10.1525/rep.2005.92.1.1.

Burkholder, Z. (2012). "Education for Citizenship in a Bi-Racial Civilization": Black Teachers and the Social Construction of Race, 1929–1954. *Journal of Social History, 46*(2), 335–363.

Charron, K. M. (2012). *Freedom's Teacher: The Life of Septima Clark*. Chapel Hill: The University of North Carolina Press.

Douglas, D. (2005). *Jim Crow Moves North: The Battle over Northern School Segregation, 1865–1954*. New York: Cambridge University Press.

Douglass, F. (1855). *My Bondage and My Freedom* ... Miller, Orton & Mulligan.

Ford, J. (2014). Close-Up: Fugitivity and the Filmic Imagination (Introduction). *Black Camera, 5*(2), 3–4. https://doi.org/10.2979/blackcamera.5.2.3

Fultz, M. (1995). African American Teachers in the South, 1890–1940: Powerlessness and the Ironies of Expectations and Protest. *History of Education Quarterly, 35*(4), 401–422.

Gilmore, G. (1996). *Gender and Jim Crow: Women and the Politics of White Supremacy in North Carolina, 1896–1920*. Chapel Hill: The University of North Carolina Press.

Givens, J. R. (2016). "A Grammar for Black Education beyond Borders": Exploring Technologies of Schooling in the African Diaspora. *Race, Ethnicity and Education, 19*(6), 1288–1302.

Givens, J. R. (2016). "He was, undoubtedly, a wonderful character": Black Teachers' Representations of Nat Turner during Jim Crow. *Souls, 18*(2–4), 215–234.

Higginbotham, E. B. (1994). *Righteous Discontent: The Women's Movement in the Black Baptist Church, 1880–1920* (Revised edition). Cambridge, MA: Harvard University Press.

John Hope Franklin Humanities Institute. (2016). *The Black Outdoors: Fred Moten and Saidiya Hartman in Conversation with J. Kameron Carter and Sarah Jane Cervenak*. Goodson Chapel, Duke Divinity School. Retrieved from https://www.youtube.com/watch?v=t_tUZ6dybrc&t=1440s.

Johnson, E. A. (1890). *A School History of the Negro Race in America from 1619 to 1890*. Raleigh : Edwards & Broughton, Printers.

Mackey, N. (1992). Other: From Noun to Verb. *Representations*, (39), 51–70.

McKissack, P. (1997). *A Picture of Freedom*. New York: Scholastic.

Moss, H. J. (2009). *Schooling Citizens the Struggle for African American Education in Antebellum America*. Chicago: University of Chicago Press.

Moten, F. (2007, October 19). "Black Optimism/Black Operation." Unpublished paper on file with the author.

Porter, D. B. (1936). The Organized Educational Activities of Negro Literary Societies, 1828–1846. *The Journal of Negro Education, 5*(4), 555–576.

Proctor, J., & Federal Writers Project. (1937). Narrative of Jenny Proctor. Retrieved from http://nationalhumanitiescenter.org/pds/maai/enslavement/text1/jennyproctor.pdf.

Roberts, N. (2015). *Freedom as Marronage*. Chicago: University of Chicago Press.

Siddle Walker, V. (1996). *Their Highest Potential: An African American School Community in the Segregated South*. Chapel Hill: The University of North Carolina Press.

Siddle Walker, V. (2018). *The Lost Education of Horace Tate: Uncovering the Hidden Heroes Who Fought for Justice in Schools*. New York: The New Press.

Thomas, G. (2006). PROUD FLESH Inter/Views: Sylvia Wynter. *ProudFlesh: New Afrikan Journal of Culture, Politics and Consciousness, 0*(4).

Tyack, D. (1974). *The One Best System: A History of American Urban Education*. Cambridge, MA: Harvard University Press.

Walker, D. (1830). *David Walker's Appeal to the Coloured Citizens of the World*. Baltimore, MD: Black Classic Press.

Watkins, W. H. (1993). Black Curriculum Orientations: A Preliminary Inquiry. *Harvard Educational Review, 63*(3), 321–38.

Watkins, W. H. (2005). *Black Protest Thought and Education*. New York: Peter Lang.

Webber, T. L. (1978). *Deep Like the Rivers: Education in the Slave Quarter Community, 1831–1865*. New York: Norton.

Williams, H. (2007). *Self-Taught: African American Education in Slavery and Freedom*. Chapel Hill: The University of North Carolina Press.

Woodson, C. G. (1915). *The Education of the Negro Prior to 1861 : A History of the Education of the Colored People of the United States from the Beginning of Slavery to the Civil War*. New York : Putnam.

Woodson, C. G. (1922). *The Negro in Our History*. Washington, DC: Associated Publishers.

Woodson, C. G. (2008). *The Mis-Education of the Negro*. Washington, DC: ASNLH.

Zimmerman, A. (2010). *Alabama in Africa: Booker T. Washington, the German Empire, and the Globalization of the New South* (Reprint edition). Princeton, NJ: Princeton University Press.

# 4

# ON LABOR AND PROPERTY

## Historically White Colleges, Black Bodies, and Constructions of (Anti) Humanity

*T. Elon Dancy and Kirsten T. Edwards*

Since its inception, the U.S. institution of higher education has been dependent on the labor of Black humans. How that labor has been interpreted and acquired throughout history has endured less than sufficient scrutiny in published scholarship. U.S. colleges and universities still must grapple with engagements of Black bodies as property. While all U.S. educational institutions participate in settler-colonial contracts, the focus on historically white institutions situates analysis on the institutional type foundational to settler-colonial color-caste systems. In this way, colleges and universities serve as not only catalyst but model for the propagation and maintenance of a "civil" society dependent on the ownership of Black bodies.

> American colleges were not innocent or passive beneficiaries of conquest and colonial slavery. The European invasion of the Americas and the modern slave trade pulled peoples throughout the Atlantic world into each others' lives, and colleges were among the colonial institutions that braided their histories and rendered their fates dependent and antagonistic. The academy never stood apart from American slavery—in fact, it stood beside church and state as the third pillar of a civilization built on bondage. (Wilder, 2013, p. xx)

To better understand the foundations of the "race as property" civil order inherent to the West, we draw on Charles Mills' *The Racial Contract*. Mills (1997) argues the sociopolitical foundation of Western society is dependent on the presence of race as a fundamental organizing principle. The perfunctory agreement that establishes expectations for moral agents in a civil society—the social contract—is predicated on an understanding that white is human, and conversely non-whites are equivalent to non-humans and are therefore excluded from participation in civil society. Mills defines this precursory exclusion as the racial contract. For Western society's social contract to thrive, for whites to be subjects of the contract, non-whites must serve as objects of the contract. Fundamental to the maintenance of US society is an ontological relationship with the non-white body as property. This social arrangement was solidified through the establishment of the settler-colonial state and ensconced through its colonial colleges.

In this chapter, we argue that these original purposes persist today, and that the 21st century Black individual who participates in U.S. post-secondary education must contend with dehumanizing perceptions of their labor that reify a subject (white) to object (Black) relationship with the institution. Further, this chapter explains how theorizations of colonialism and anti-Blackness (re)interpret the arrangement between these universities, in particular, and Black bodies. To assist in this analysis, we explore three dimensions of anti-blackness as manifested within higher education: 1) interpretations of Black labor through colonial arrangements, 2) relationship between labor, ownership, and education, and 3) institutionalization of Black suffering.

## The Colony and Black Labor

"Y'all can't do this!" H shouted. "I'm free!" he said. "I'm a free man!"

"Naw," the pit boss said. He looked at H carefully and pulled out a knife from the inside of his coat. He began to sharpen the knife against an ironstone he kept on his desk. "No such thing as a free nigger." (Excerpt from *Homegoing* by Yaa Gyasi)

Settler colonialism is a practice of direct global domination, which involves the subjugation of one people to another (Fanon, 1961). The term colonialism is frequently used to describe the European settlements of North America, Australia, New Zealand, Algeria, and Brazil. Settler colonialism describes a process in which colonialists emigrate(d) with the express purposes of building a new community through territorial occupation (Russell, 2001). Eliminating Indigenous people, pilfering land, and creating new wealth systems from the built and rebuilt environment are fundamental organizing principles of the settler-colonial project (Wolfe, 2006). European settlers colonized the U.S. vis-à-vis a number of terrorist acts on aboriginal inhabitants including disease, broken treaties and outright massacre (Mills, 1997). Settler colonization was a process driven by capitalist impulses, which also sought to institute settler political, cultural, and economic hegemony managed vis-à-vis a network of relations between "metropolitan officials" (Veracini, 2010).

Sets of practices aimed at domination. The settler colonialists raised questions about whether all were members of the same human species or "family of man" (Omi & Winant, 2010, p. 14). Europeans used interpretations of Judeo-Christian doctrine to devalue Indigenous humanity and assume spiritual ineptness (Omi & Winant, 2010). This interpretation drove the philosophy behind who should be free, who should own, who should be eliminated, and who should be enslaved (Omi & Winant, 2010). The Europeans distinguished human beings from "others" or "humanoids" through seizing land, the denial of political rights, the introduction of indentured servitude, enslavement, other forms of coercive labor, and complete extermination.

While the U.S. settler colony saw a period of white indentured servitude, Blackness became a formal marker of chattel enslavement. Servants understood as white experienced limited loss of liberty but people understood as Black were enslaved for life. While servant status could not descend to offspring, Black children took the status of the mother. In *Capitalism and Slavery*, Williams (1994) elaborates that skin color and phenotype differences made it easier to justify and rationalize Black enslavement, "to exact the mechanical obedience of a plough-ox or a cart-horse" (p. 19), and to subjugate Black people using the various oppressive tools that made "slave labor" possible. The enslavement of Black people must also be understood in the context of capitalist motivations. Williams (1944) adds:

> The Negro slave was cheaper. The money which procured a white man's services for ten years could buy a Negro for life. As the governor of Barbados stated, the Barbadian planters found by experience that "three Blacks work better and cheaper than one white." Here, then, is the origin of Negro slavery. The reason was economic, not racial; it had to do not with the color of the laborer, but the cheapness of the labor. As compared with Indian and white labor, Negro slavery was eminently superior … The features of the man, his hair, color, and dentifrice, his "subhuman" characteristics so widely pleaded were only the latter rationalizations to justify a simple economic fact: that the colonies needed labor and resorted to Negro labor because it was cheapest and best. (pp. 19–20)

Mills (1997) discusses the emergent color-caste system and its legacies in terms of the racial contract, or the set of relationships and conditions that must occur to maintain white supremacy, or the white settler-colonial state. All whites are beneficiaries of the contract, though some whites are not signatories to it. At the center of this contract are agreements that define a white class as superior and various subsets of human beings as "nonwhite" and therefore a different, inferior status. The general purpose of the contract is always the differential privileging of white people as a group among non-whites and the exploitation of their bodies, land, and resources. The use of narrative is a critical condition in the racial contract. Mills (1997) explains the ways in which whiteness narrates itself as default human:

> The establishment of society ... implies the denial that a society already existed; the creation of society requires the intervention of white men, who are thereby positioned as already sociopolitical beings. White men who are (definitionally) already part of society encounter nonwhites who are not, who are "savage" residents of a state of nature characterized in terms of wilderness, jungle, wasteland ... In the colonial case, admittedly preexisting but (for one reason or another) deficient societies (decadent, stagnant, corrupt) are taken over and run for the "benefit" of the nonwhite natives, who are deemed childlike, incapable of self-rule and handling their own affairs, and thus appropriately wards of the state ... the Racial Contract establishes a racial polity, a racial state, and a racial juridical system, where the status of whites and nonwhites is clearly demarcated, whether by law or custom. And the purpose of this state ... is ... specifically to maintain and reproduce this racial order, securing the privileges and advantages of the full white citizens and maintaining the subordination of nonwhites. (pp. 13–14)

The term postcolonialism is a way some scholars have named ongoing settler-colonial projects, including racial contracts, or the residual political, socio-economic, and psychological legacies and effects that persist despite some dismantling of colonial control. As the authors of *The Empire Writes Back* (1989) elaborate,

> We use the term "post-colonial" ... to cover all the culture affected by the imperial process from the moment of colonization to the present day. This is because there is a continuity of preoccupations throughout the historical process initiated by European imperial aggression. (p. 2)

Although U.S. institutions claim "advancement" following several events (e.g., the Civil War, Brown v. Board of Education 1954, Civil Rights Act of 1964) concerned with authentic enactment of what the U.S. constitution espouses about "equality," racialized realities continue to materialize in daily life. Hence, a postcolonial framing is at best a way of naming the continuity of colonial preoccupations after these events and in no way suggests colonial demise. The "postcolonial" character of these institutions remains the maintenance of the colonial purpose: to fulfill white elite male capitalist ambitions and dominate all other groups in pursuit of this goal (Mills, 1997).

Anti-Blackness is essential to the colonial aim and, as a central concern and proposition within Afro-pessimism (Dumas, 2016) issues a critique on Black domination as unresolvable through "reforms" and only called into question with "absolute violence" (Fanon, 1961, p. 37). Afro-pessimism theorizes that Black people exist in a structurally antagonistic relationship with humanity (Wilderson, 2010). The Black cannot be human and is not simply an "other" but is other than human. Hence, matters of exploitation and alienation are not central ways of knowing "The Black" as those positionalities preserve humanness. Rather, Blackness is predicated on "modalities of accumulation and fungibility" (the collection and manageability of property or things). In conversation with postcolonialism's theorization of colonialism as uncured, anti-Blackness names the ways in which the technologies and imaginations that allow a social recognition of the humanness of others systematically excludes this possibility for Black people (Dumas, 2016). The violence of the Middle Passage and the slave estate have not ended; rather, the violence "[recomposes] and [reenacts] their horrors upon each succeeding generation of Blacks" (Wilderson, 2010, p. 3). This condition of Black "life" means Jim Crow, the ghetto, the prison industrial complex, school-to-prison pipelines comprise a continuum of structural violence.

Anti-Blackness is reproduced through two specific institutional arrangements that enable Black subjugation (enslavements): the extraction of labor from the Black body without engaging the body as a laborer but as property and Black subjections, or the mechanisms (e.g., stereotypical narratives) that institutions use to police, control, imprison, and kill. Work is not structured as an organic principle for "a slave" (Wilderson, 2010). U.S. institutions objectively positioned the Black body against work, outside and against the wage relation. In other words, to be "free," to be a worker or laborer, or any combination of the two was negatively defined in relation to the "slave" (R. L., 2013). Following emancipation, Black bodies were situated outside the constraints of wage labor. Because the "slave" has no relationship to work, the slave is in need of labor discipline (coercive and enforced arrangements institutions used to construct consent). During the period of U.S. industrialization in the 19th century, labor contracts with an impoverished submissive Black working class maintained slave-owning labor management techniques (Hartman, 1997). Hence, industries and factories sustain lines of continuity from the plantation system.

Anti-Blackness holds that the Black is not only outside a relational being framework but is always-already property. In the Dred Scott v. Sandford decision, Justice Taney wrote:

> [T]he public history of every European nation displays it in a manner too plain to be mistaken. They had for more than a century before been regarded as beings of an inferior order, and altogether unfit to associate with the white race, either in social or political relations; and so far inferior, that they had no rights which the white man was bound to respect; and that the negro might justly and lawfully to slavery for his benefit. He

was bought and sold, and treated as an ordinary article of merchandise and traffic, whenever a profit could be made by it … And in no nation was this opinion more firmly fixed or more uniformly acted upon than by the English Government and English people. They not only seized them on the coast of Africa, and sold them or held them in slavery for their own use. But they took them as ordinary articles of merchandise. (Banks, 2017)

The decision in the Dred Scott is clear: the status does not change simply because one's "owner" relinquishes property rights. Black peoples remain property whether or not an individual owns them. Justice Daniel's concurring opinion also reflects an understanding of Africa as ontologically colonized or always-already the property of Europe which erases Africa as a land of nations colonized by Europe. As Smith (2014) notes, the narrative that Africa is always the property of Europe consequently constructs Black people and their struggles against the colonial state as always the internal property of the United States:

> [A]nti-Black struggle must be contained within a domesticated anti-racist framework that cannot challenge the settler state itself. Why, for example, is Martin Luther King, Jr. always described as a civil rights leader rather than anti-colonial organizer, despite his clear anti-colonial organizing against the war in Vietnam? Through anti-Blackness, not only are Black peoples rendered the property of the settler state, but Black struggle itself remains its property—solely containable within the confines of the settler state. (p. 3)

Settler-colonial constructions of labor and property are essential to understanding the irrational design in anti-Blackness. For instance, the rationales in Johnson v. McIntosh (1823) and Lowe v. United States (1902) established that Indigenous peoples, as "incompetent," "savages" and non-discoverers of themselves, did not constitute workers and hence they could not create property nor acquire a domicile. It is here that Black people's existential reality poses a fundamental contradiction for the settler-colonial state (Smith, 2014). The justification for colonialism was predicated upon an understanding that settlers labored but Indigenous people did not. Not only does this decision erase Indigenous labor it also erases Black labor by defining whites as the laborers at the same time they relied on an unseen, unrecognized Black labor. Accordingly, the decisions in both court cases suggest that Black people's work cannot constitute labor under settler colonialism because only labor can create property. The labor of Black people, who were already defined as property, cannot therefore create property for Black people (Smith, 2014).

Anti-Blackness as a framework also extends beyond the construction of the Black body as property. The notion of Black fungibility describes the ways in which settler colonialists use Black bodies as symbols, signifiers, and means to settle space and expand territories. The space-making practices of settler colonialism require the production of the Black body as a fungible (exchangeable or replaceable) form of property. For instance, In Scenes of Subjection, Saidiya Hartman argues that the enslaved embody the abstract "interchangeability and replaceability" that is endemic to the commodity (Hartman, 1997, p. 21). Further, what Hartman names as "figurative capacities of blackness," allows the Settler-Master to conceptualize Blackness as the ultimate sign for expansion and unending space within the symbolic economy of settlement (Hartman, 1997, p. 7). Blackness is much more than labor within both slavery's and settler colonialism's imaginaries; it signals opportunities for accumulation and white possibilities.

The present chapter argues that the perpetuation of an anti-Black settler-colonial design is not by happenstance, but is instead a deliberate manifestation of the white supremacist social and material practices (Wilderson, 2010; Ani, 1994). The degradation and denial of Black life within higher education is a necessary (re)articulation of enslavement. Thus, how does this settler-colonial reality manifest within colleges and universities? What does it mean for a system of higher education to maintain an ontoepistemological relationship of slavery with Black people? These are significant questions to ask as they compel scholars to think deeply about the colonial state. To be sure, there is much academic discussion about bias, discrimination, and diversity that distract from the specific institutional arrangements that enabled Black subjections to continue. The authors of this chapter contend that an examination of anti-Blackness and the ways in which white identity is predicated on ownership of and violence against Black bodies is inextricably connected to the propagation of effective anticolonial Black resistance within post-secondary education.

## Labor, Ownership, and Higher Education

In *Ebony and Ivy: Race, Slavery, and the Troubled History of America's Universities*, Wilder (2013) dispels the notion that there were no Black people in colonial colleges. In fact, enslaved Black people outnumbered faculty, administrators, and trustees at a number of Ivy League colleges, like Dartmouth for instance (Wilder, 2013). Black people erected the buildings, cooked the food, and cleaned the dormitories yet were engaged in the objective. Colonizers advocated (from college campus podiums) for the inhumane treatment of Black people everywhere, and violence was a common experience for the enslaved on college campuses. Colonial college trustees (many of whom were ministers) tortured and murdered enslaved Black men, women, and children in the most sadistic ways.

College presidents, many of whom were "slave masters," used enslaved Black people as personal attendants and as house servants to maintain the president's mansion. Harvard president Increase Mather (from 1692 to 1701), used an enslaved man "gifted" to him by his son Cotton Mather, to run errands for the college. Harvard president Benjamin Wadsworth (1725–1737) brought an enslaved man named Titus, who lived with his family, to the college and "bought a Negro Wench" two days before arriving on campus. Benjamin Franklin, founder of the College of Philadelphia; the first eight presidents of the College of New Jersey (Princeton); and Georgetown presidents Fathers Louis William Valentin DuBourg (1796–1798) and Stephen L. Dubuisson (1825–1826), as Wilder's (2013) research highlights, all accumulated enslaved Black people for their own personal service during their tenures as the top college administrator.

The residue of these colonial labor relations persist within the contemporary institution. Several scholars have explored the differentiated labor expectations placed on Black academics (Brown, 2012; Burgess, 1997; Gregory, 1999; Patitu & Hinton, 2003; Thomas & Hollenshead, 2001). These expectations come in the form of increased mentoring and advising, committee work, scrutiny and subsequent dismissal of culturally relevant scholarship, among other demands. As previously mentioned, there is clear evidence and discussion of "discriminatory" practice. However, fewer scholars have connected these discrepancies to colonial design (Dancy, 2014; Edwards, 2010, 2013; Wagner, Acker, & Mayuzumi, 2008; Wane, Jagire, & Murad, 2013). Recognizing anti-Black settler colonialism reveals not simply a trend of exclusionary practice, but instead a performance of inclusion that reasserts the colonial order and engages the Black body as property.

For example, the labor expectations placed on Black women are not just comparatively excessive; they are reflective of domestic servitude and eroticism (Austin, 1995; Edwards, 2014; Harley, 2007). Black women academics are expected to attend to the caregiving needs of not only students of color, but white students and faculty. They are also regularly called upon to attend to the failures of whites, or "clean up behind," through interim positions, promotion following scandal, committee leadership, and assumptions of curricular leniency. These colonial labors are often uncompensated and unseen. When Black women insist on the recognition of their labor or resist accommodating white student mediocrity, they are summarily punished as defiant Sapphires (Austin, 1995). Black women's theoretical contributions are also rarely acknowledged. When they are, it is within very narrowly defined curricular parameters, and is often experienced by white audiences as provocative and momentarily titillating, but not central to U.S. higher education mission and purpose (Edwards, 2014; Fasching-Varner, 2009).

Black male bodies on college campuses are seen as primarily generators of income and properties of entertainment (Dancy, 2012; Rhoden, 2006; R. L.,

2013). The testimonies of Black male non-student-athletes attest to the academy's rejection of Black men as intellectual, and not primarily corporal occupants. Black males across historically white campuses lament the regular assumption that their admission is predicated on their athletic prowess (Dancy, 2012; Harper, 2015; Palmer, Wood, Dancy, & Strayhorn, 2014; Strayhorn, 2008). For a Black man to exist within higher education as a thinking being is oxymoronic in the white psyche. A comparative analysis of political commentary regarding legacy, athletic, and affirmative action admissions confirms the academy's commitment to white entitlement, Black male bodies as commodity, and the rejection of Black intellect (Charles, Fischer, Mooney, 2009). For Black people, inclusion within anti-Black settler-colonial institutions of higher education is not simply the experience of discrimination, but primarily white insistence on the practice of enslavement.

Another essential component of the colonial project is seducing the colonized into the fruitless effort that is modeling white humanity (Fanon, 1952/2008; Memmi, 1965/1991; Mbembe, 2001). This practice of striving for an elusive and impossible goal works to reaffirm the humanity of the colonizer. Higher education is one of the primary sites where this seduction takes place. As Samuels (2004) argues, education, along with science and law, is one of the deities of U.S. democracy. In the present and recent past, colonial discourse has framed education as fundamental to achieving the "American Dream," and thus white humanity. However, for non-white, especially Black, national occupants the pursuit of full sociopolitical participation by way of educational institutions has proven to be a dream deferred (Edwards, 2011; Hughes, 1987). Continued disparities in institutional funding, attrition, tenure and promotion, executive leadership, and support reflect the fallacy of a truly post (or beyond)-colonial institution embracing of a multicultural humanity.

National rhetoric may have shifted to publicly disavow discrimination and injustice; however, the lack of shift in foundational values and design exposes the propagandized nature of "liberty and justice for all." To be clear, the present chapter seeks to focus its gaze into the system, the settler-colonial project scholars are "hooded into" that is fundamentally committed to a sociopolitical vision of domination via anti-Blackness. We, therefore, take seriously Woodson's (1933/2000) critique of white educational institutions as committed to the intellectual, psychological, and social destruction of Black life. Fanon (1961) illustrates:

> Perhaps … sufficiently demonstrat[ing] that colonialism is not simply content to impose its rule upon the present and the future of a dominated country. Colonialism is not satisfied merely with hiding a people in its grip and emptying the native's brain of all form and content. By a kind of perverted logic, it turns to the past of the oppressed people, and distorts, disfigures and destroys it. (p. 37).

By distorting the past of colonized peoples, as well as their historical relationship with settler colonialism, white supremacy not only justifies the imposition of a Eurocentric logic on educational practice, but it also erases Black intellectual traditions and denies the trauma of the Black experience as essential curricular content.

Current academic standards are inextricably linked to the perpetuation of white supremacy and white interests. Pedagogical practice and objectives are constructed to support an epistemic orientation to the world that is Eurocentric. For instance, positivist assumptions about objectivity and postpositivist reliance on Descartian perspectives of the thinking (disembodied) man support anthropological and consumptive approaches to engagement with the Other (Baszile, 2008; Lowe, Byron, & Mennicke, 2014; Minh-ha, 1989; Spivak, 1988; Talburt & Stewart, 1999; Thomas, 2013). When students and faculty of color struggle to align their intellectual and sociopolitical realities to the pedagogical practice, they are dismissed as inferior. An individual's proximity to "humanity" is directly dependent on their ability to manifest (white) destiny. Further, the prioritization of a white supremacist logic as institutional design is both curricular and co-curricular emerging in and beyond the classroom. The athletic field is possibly the starkest example of co-curricular anti-Blackness.

## Black Suffering as Institutional Outcomes

Essential in white supremacist settler-colonial educational design, Black fungibility manifests violence-effect in positionalities of Black and white people on college campuses (Wilderson, 2010; Hartman, 1997). As Wilderson notes, the spectacles of the plantation "slave" parties and weddings, musical performances of the enslaved for "masters," scenes of "intimacy" and "seduction" between Black women and white men cannot be disentangled from the "gratuitousness of violence" that structures Black suffering (Wilderson, 2010: p. 46). From discursive acts of "love" or "respect" to whippings and rapes, white engagement of the captive Black body is always sutured to a structural suffering in which Black people's speech and mobility are incapacitated. Because the Black body is fungible, or exchangeable and adaptable, the engagement can appear loving, even humane, but the white psyche still engages the Black body as property, albeit enjoyable. This analysis is particularly stark in white celebrations of Black athletic triumphs on football field and basketball court sites. U.S. college student affairs units must also grapple with the construction of the Black body as property.

Inducing the humiliation and suffering of Black people for sport comprises the early student life in the colonial colleges. These practices were necessary to mark the separation between Black people and whites. For example, at Williams College, several college students (who were all white and male) forced a Black man to smash his own head into wooden boards and barrels for their entertainment (Wilder, 2013). On other early college campuses, college students shot at Black enslaved children to satisfy their boredom when out of class. At one of the Yale campuses, the record shows that the early students raped Black women so frequently, the college removed them from the students' presence except the cook whom the students also terrorized.

Early on, white educational institutions recognized and facilitated one of the defining principles of anti-Blackness: the negation of Black humanity by way of violence. Dumas (2016) argues,

> Black people exist in a structurally antagonistic relationship with [white frames of] humanity ... antiblackness marks an irreconcilability between the Black and any sense of social or cultural regard ... [antiblackness necessitates] utter contempt for, and acceptance of violence against the Black. (p. 13)

Colonial students, faculty, and staff understood that white humanity is dependent on its ability to harm Black life. To avoid violence against Black people would place white humanity in question, because in an anti-Black polity, white humanity is predicated on Black inhumanity. Subsequently, the Black enslavement was maintained by physical, sexual, and psychological brutality, followed by the reign of Jim Crow which was established through the terrorization of Black communities.

Within contemporary higher education, these configurations of anti-Black violence continue. While physical insecurity is less evident, psychological and economic vulnerabilities persist. Theories such as microaggressions, tokenism, impostorship, and racial battle fatigue attest to the psychological torment repeatedly visited upon Black humanity in higher education (Dancy, 2014; Hotchkins & Dancy, 2017; Dancy & Jean-Marie, 2014; Hotchkins, 2016; Smith, 2014). Regular patterns of Black student protest reveal a culture of white antagonism on college campuses (Johnston, 2015). The continued defunding of historically Black colleges and universities (HBCUs) reflects a sordid commitment to the elimination of Black enterprise. It also undergirds the relationship of trauma between Blackness and the educational system; a relationship HBCUs play a protective role against. In many ways, HBCUs are the contemporary manifestation of Underground Railroad safe houses. While not beyond a critique of settler-colonial strivings, they have also protected and supported Black students along their journey to educational and economic freedom amidst a dangerous environment. Defunding exposes the state's commitment to Black vulnerability.

In these settler-colonial relationships, Black resistance and despair is understood as not only a nuisance, but also a public display of Black suffering for the consumption of a white audience (Alexander, 1995). Black suffering decorates the landscape of white humanity. It cannot be responded to with understanding and empathy. Instead it is Black full intellectual participation in higher education that is illegible, accumulated (collected), exchangeable, and openly vulnerable (Anzaldúa, 1981; Wilderson, 2010). Black academics are not subalterns but the property (slaves) of their colleagues (Wilderson, 2010).

Assaults on Black humanity in high-revenue university athletics provide a lens into the continuity of plantation, or slave estate politics (Hartman, 1997). Interrogating the experiences of Black people through an anti-Blackness framework requires reckoning with them, not as subalterns, but as the slaves of athletic directors and coaches. The following section pays specific attention to this and the ways in which historically white institutions maintain anti-Blackness through managing Black bodies as property, utilizing tools of property accumulation, fungibility, and violence.

## Afropessimist Reflections, Afrocentric Rebellions: Beyond Black Educational Death

What the reinterpretations of data reveal is that white higher education perpetuates a cycle of colonial preoccupations predicated on the negation of Black humanity. Anti-Blackness is not simply an unfortunate characteristic of historically white institutions, but fundamental to their identity and perpetuation. Frankly stated, for historically white colleges and universities to continue to exist as they do, they must enact anti-Black violence. If Black scholars take seriously an Afropessimist analysis that situates colleges and universities as agents of the settler-colonial polity, what is a logical course of action moving forward?

The authors note two possible pathways for Black resistance. The first pathway involves intra-institutional action, which seems to be the most common action taken by Black scholars. Unfortunately, we also note that much resistance that happens within the institution does not take seriously anti-Blackness and Black social death within the gaze of those who believe themselves to be white. Through an Afropessimist analysis, we imagine what intra-institutional resistance could look like. Intra-institutional resistance within this frame would target the creation of policy that acknowledged and maintained the health of Black life. Relatedly, action would recognize and dismantle whiteness. Resistors would not be distracted by cosmetic change, but would insist on structural analyses that identify white interests predicated on Black death. For instance, debates on college campuses concerning the free speech right of white supremacists to verbally assault and undermine Black life, would go beyond examinations of civil discourse and would interrogate the ways in which the first amendment as well as Western constructions of civility are beholden to a conception of humanity as white, and subsequently the degradation of Black life. Therefore, only white people have access to the right to civil free speech, while also enjoying protection from its abuses. In fact, according to Mills, the objectification of Black life is the necessary component that concretizes the right to free speech in a white supremacist civil society. Analyses such as these must remain at the center of intra-institutional resistance movements.

We also recognize that people who believe themselves to be white regularly dismiss as illogical arguments that bring into question the logic of white supremacy. Further, white supremacy has a long history of denying the ontology of Black resistance (Fanon, 1952/2008). As such, the second pathway we propose is possibly the most tenable: divestment. What would it mean for Black people to abandon all hope in partaking in the white social contract? What would it mean for Black people to refuse to exist as object or subject in settler-colonial arrangements? The present chapter challenges the reader to consider the possibilities of Black divestment, Black total abandonment of white interests. We, the authors, envision a divestment politic as the logical bridge between an Afropessimist present and Afrocentric future. As Ani (1994) notes,

> Now that we have broken the power of their ideology, we must leave them and direct our energies toward the recreation of cultural alternatives informed by ancestral visions of a future that celebrates our Africaness and encourages the best of the human spirit. (p. 570)

As Afropessimism analyses have taught us, Black social death and anti-Black violence are inextricably linked to the maintenance of a white civil society. With this reality in mind, the present chapter encourages readers to begin envisaging strategies that un-suture Black life from white frames towards an Afrocentric future. The Black future awaits these possibilities.

# References

Alexander, E. (1995). "Can you be BLACK and look at this?": Reading the Rodney King video(s). *Public Culture*, 7, 77–94.

Ani, M. (1994). *Yurugu: An Afrikan-Centered Critique of European Cultural Thought and Behavior*. Washington, DC: Nkonimfo Publications.

Anzaldúa, G. (1981). Speaking in Tongues: A Letter to 3rd World Women Writers. In C. Moraga & G. Anzaldúa (Eds.), *This Bridge Called My Back: Writings by Radical Women of Color* (pp. 165–174). New York: Kitchen Table: Women of Color Press.

Ashcroft, B., Griffiths, G., & Tiffin, H. (1989). *The Empire Writes Back: Theory and Practice in Post-colonial Literatures*. London: Routledge.

Austin, R. (1995). Sapphire Bound! In K. Crenshaw, N. Gotanda, G. Peller & K. Thomas (Eds.), *Critical Race Theory: The Key Writings that Formed the Movement* (pp. 426–437). New York: The New Press.

Banks, C. F. (2017). *The State and Federal Courts: A Complete Guide to History, Powers, and Controversy*. Santa Barbara, CA: ABC-Clio.

Baszile, D. T. (2006). In This Place where I Don't Quite Belong: Claiming the Ontoepistemological In-between. In T. R. Berry & N. D. Mizelle (Eds.), *From Oppression to Grace: Women of Color and Their Dilemmas within the Academy* (pp. 195–208). Sterling, VA: Stylus Publishing.

Brown, A. J. B. (2012). Black Women Faculty in Predominantly White Space: Negotiating Discourses of Diversity. In M. Christian (Ed.), *Integrated but Unequal: Black
Faculty in Predominately White Space* (pp. X–X). Trenton, NJ: Africa World Press.

Burgess, N. J. (1997). Tenure and Promotion among African American Women in the
Academy: Issues and Strategies. In L. Benjamin (Ed.), *Black Women in the Academy:
Promises and Perils* (pp. 227–235). Gainesville, FL: University Press of Florida.

Dancy, T. E. & Brown, M. C. (2011). The mentoring and induction of educators of
color: Addressing the impostor syndrome in academe. *Journal of School Leadership*,
21(4), 607–634.

Dancy, T. E. & Jean-Marie, G. (2014). Faculty of color in higher education: Exploring
the intersections of identity, impostorship, and internalized racism. *Mentoring and
Tutoring: Partnership in Learning Journal*, 22(4), 354–372.

DuBois, W.E.B. (1903). *The Souls of Black Folk*. Chicago, IL: A. C. McClurg.

Dumas, M. J. (2016). Against the dark: Antiblackness in education policy and discourse.
*Theory Into Practice*, 55, 11–19.

Edwards, K. T. (2010). Incidents in the life of Kirsten T. Edwards: A personal examination
of the academic in-between space. *Journal of Curriculum Theorizing*, 26(1), 113–128.

Edwards, K. T. (2011). Maybe Langston was right? *Journal of Curriculum and Pedagogy*,
8(1), 22–25.

Edwards, K. T. (2014). Teach with me: The promise of a raced politic for social justice
in college classrooms. *Journal of Critical Thought and Praxis*, 2(2), 1–20. http://lib.
dr.iastate.edu/jctp/vol2/iss2/3/.

Fanon, F. (1952/2008). *Black Skin, White Masks*. New York: Grove Press.

Fanon, F. (1961). *The Wretched of the Earth*. New York: Grove Press.

Fasching-Varner, K. J. (2009). No! The team ain't alright! The institutional and individual problematics of race. *Social Identities*, 15(6), 811–829.

Gregory, S. T. (1999). *Black Women in the Academy: The Secrets to Success and Achievement*.
Lanham, MD: University Press of America.

Harley, D. A. (2007). Maids of academe: African American women faculty at predominately white institutions. *Journal of African American Studies*, 12(1), 19–36.

Harper, S. R. (2015). Black male college achievers and resistant responses to racist
stereotypes at predominantly white colleges and universities. *Harvard Educational
Review*, 85(4), 646–674.

Hawkins, B. J. (2010a). Economic recession, college athletics, and issues of diversity and
inclusion: When White America sneezes, Black America catches pneumonia. *Journal
of Intercollegiate Athletics*, 3(1), 96–100.

Hawkins, B. J. (2010b). *The New Plantation: Black Athletes, College Sports, and Predominantly White NCAA Institutions*. New York: Palgrave Macmillan.

Hotchkins, B. & Dancy, T. F. (2017). A house is not a home: Black students' responses
to racism in university residential halls. *Journal of College and University Housing*,
43(3), 43–53.

Hughes, G. (2013). Racial Justice, hegemony, and bias incidents in American higher
education. Sociology and Anthropology Faculty Publications. Paper 22. http://
scholarship.richmond.edu/cgi/viewcontent.cgi?article=1022&context=socanth-
faculty-publications/.

Hughes, L. (1987). *Selected poems of Langston Hughes*. New York: Vintage Books (Original work published 1959).

*Increasing Access, Retention, and Persistence in Higher Education* (3rd ed., Vol. 40, JB Higher
and Adult Education Series). San Francisco, CA: Jossey-Bass.

Johnston, A. (2015). Student protests, then and now: From "Hey, hey, LBJ!" to "Black Lives Matter!" *The Chronicle of Higher Education*. Retrieved from https://www. chronicle.com/article/Student-Protests-ThenNow/234542.

L., R. (2013, June/July). Wanderings of the slave: Black life and social death. Retrieved October 13, 2016, from www.metamute.org/editorial/articles/wanderings-slave-black-life-and-social-death/.

Lowe, M., Byron, R., Mennicke, S. (2014). The racialized impact of study abroad on US students' subsequent interracial relations. *Educational Research International*, 1–9.

Mbembe, A. (2001). *On the Postcolony*. Berkeley, CA: University of California Press.

Memmi, A. (1965/1991). *The Colonizer and the Colonized*. Boston, MA: Beacon Press.

Mills, C. (1997). *The Racial Contract*. Ithaca, NY: Cornell University Press.

Minh-ha, T. (1989). *Woman Native Other*. Bloomington and Indianapolis, IN: Indiana University Press.

Omi, M. & Winant, H. (2010). Racial Formations. In Rothberg, P. (Ed.), *Race, Class, and Gender in the United States* (pp. 13–22). New York: Worth Publishers.

Palmer, R. T., Wood, J. L., Dancy, T. E., & Strayhorn, T. L. (2014). *Black Male Collegians: Increasing Access, Retention, and Persistence in Higher Education* (3rd ed., Vol. 40, JB Higher and Adult Education Series). San Francisco, CA: Jossey-Bass.

Patitu, C. L., & Hinton, K. G. (2003). The experiences of African American women faculty and administrators in higher education: Has anything changed? *New Directions for Student Services*, 104, 79–93.

Rhoden, W. C. (2006). *Forty Million-Dollar Slaves: The Rise, Fall, and Redemption of the Black Athlete*. New York: Crown.

Russell, L. (Ed.) (2001). *Colonial Frontiers: Indigenous European Encounters in Settler Societies*. Manchester: Manchester University Press.

Samuels, A. L. (2004). *Is Separate Unequal? Black Colleges and the Challenge to Desegregation*. Lawrence, KS: University Press of Kansas.

Smith, V. (2014/1788/1835). *A Narrative of the Life and Adventure of Venture: A Native of Africa, but Resident above Sixty Years in the United States of America. Related by Himself.* New London: Published by a Descendant of Venture.

Spivak, G. C. (1988). Can the Subaltern Speak? In C. Nelson & L. Grossbeg (Eds.), *Marxism and the Interpretation of Culture* (pp. 271–316). Urbana and Chicago: University of Illinois Press.

Strayhorn, T. L. (2008). The role of supportive relationships in facilitating African American males success in college. *NASPA Journal*, 1, 26–48.

Talburt, S., & Stewart, M. A. (1999). What's the subject of study abroad?: Race, gender, and "living culture". *The Modern Language Journal*, 83(2), 163–175.

Thomas, G. D., & Hollenshead, C. (2001). Resisting from the margins: The coping strategies of Black women and other women of color faculty members at a research university. *The Journal of Negro Education*, 70(3), 166–175.

Thomas, M. (2013). The problematization of racial/ethnic minority student participation in American study abroad. *Applied Linguistics Review*, 4(2), 365–390.

Veracini, L. (2010). Population. *Settler Colonialism*, 16–52.

Wagner, A., Acker, S., Mayuzumi, K. (2008). *Whose University is it, Anyway? Power and Privilege on Gendered Terrain*. Toronto, ON: Sumach Press.

Wane, N., Jagire, J., Murad, Z. (2013). *Ruptures: Anti-colonial & anti-racist feminist theorizing*. The Netherlands: Sense Publishers.

Wilder, C. S. (2013). *Ebony & Ivy: Race, Slavery, and the Troubled History of America's Universities*. New York: Bloomsbury Press.

Wilderson, F. B. (2010). *Red, White & Black: Cinema and the Structure of U.S. Antagonisms*. Durham, NC: Duke University Press.

Williams, E. E. (1994/1944). *Capitalism & Slavery*. Chapel Hill: University of North Carolina Press.

Wolfe, P. (2006). Settler colonialism and the elimination of the native. *Journal of Genocide Research*, 8(4), 387–409.

Woodson, C. G. (1933/2012). *Mis-education of the Negro*. North Chelmsford, MA: Courier Corporation.

# 5

# BLACK SPACE IN EDUCATION

## Fugitive Resistance in the Afterlife of School Segregation

*kihana miraya ross*

In the fall of 1998, I began my first semester as an undergraduate at UC Berkeley. After nearly dropping out of high school, I took a year off to wait tables (I see you Chevys) and regroup from what were a pretty traumatic four years prior (broke folks' sojourn I suppose). So in that fall of 1998, one of my classes was African American Studies R1A (a class I would teach at Berkeley years later), and my instructor was none other than Frank Wilderson III himself, a graduate student at the time in rhetoric and film studies. While I won't recount the details of that classroom here, I will say that in many ways, I began the becoming of myself in that space we created together—a space of rage, of melancholy, and of a bitter sweetness in what I have come to call *Black educational fugitive space*. And here I am, nearly 20 years later, one of those strange Black people in the academy (Hartman & Wilderson, 2003), still becoming, still grappling with living in social death (Sexton, 2011).

There are many parts to that grappling, many parts that I have yet to find adequate words for. Many parts I've stopped trying to find the words for. In our current historical moment, technology has often exacerbated that grappling, where Black death loops in a tragic screenplay, scored with the wails of childless mothers and the entitled indifference of our murderers. And yet, despite this repeated display of gratuitous violence, I long ago relinquished any inkling I had toward disbelief, toward shock or incredulity, and settled into an eerie horror, a blood-thirsty imaginary, a wretched knowing.

As an education scholar, I've long tried to find the words to articulate that wretched knowing, to adequately explicate what it means for "us" to attend "they schools" (Dead Prez, 2000). Oftentimes, I return to that space we created in Frank's class—to many of the ideas, feelings, and theoretical tools we now call Afro-pessimism. I return to that space because in the midst of the unimaginable pain of being born into death (Moten, 2013), there is also a freedom in the possibilities that death creates. Wilderson once said, with the utmost sincerity, "I'm interested in doing theoretical work that helps Black people shit on the inspiration of the entire world" (Wilderson, 2015). In other words, this world as we know it, as we exist in it, as it exists in us, is utterly debilitating in its violence, in its daily discursive and literal assassination of our being. But "what kinds of possibilities for rupture might be opened up" (Sharpe, 2016, p. 7) when we confront the realities of antiblackness in schools?

While admittedly ambitious, in this chapter I want to introduce two paradigm shifts in the way we conceive of Black education, and conceptualize what it means to be a Black student in U.S. public schools. The first is what I am calling *the afterlife of school segregation*. Similar to the critical race theory tenet that posits racism is normal (as opposed to an anomaly) within society (Delgado, 1995), or the BlackCrit framing that suggests antiblackness is endemic to how we make sense of human life (Dumas & ross, 2016), the afterlife of school segregation is a more specific rendering of Hartman's (2007) afterlife of slavery, and centers the ways in which despite the end of legal segregation of schooling, Black students remain systematically dehumanized and positioned as uneducable. The second is *Black educational fugitive space*, which has grown out of my own experiences as a Black girl (and woman) in U.S. public schools and university, and in my own praxis as a teacher of Black children and as a researcher with Black students, educators, and families. I have seen it constructed in exclusively Black places (all Black classrooms for example), in hostile takeovers, where we make space ours regardless of racial non-exclusivity (Frank's classroom for example), and in the proverbial Black head nod. Without boxing Black space, for our purposes here, I want to offer Black educational fugitive space as the ways Black students and educators enact educational fugitivity through the social production of Black space in the margin. I want to propose Black educational fugitive space manifests as both departure and refuge from the gratuitous violence of the afterlife of school segregation, and spawns the possibilities for rebirth and resistance.

## The Afterlife of School Segregation

In the "Position of the unthought" (2003), Hartman challenges a linear progress narrative of history, particularly the slavery-to-freedom paradigm, and articulates freedom as "the potentiality between the no longer and the not yet" (192). Here Hartman expounds on what she would eventually call "the afterlife of slavery" (2007), a theory that recognizes the ways "the entanglements of slavery and freedom trouble facile notions of progress that endeavor to erect absolute distinctions between bondage and liberty" (Hartman, 1997, p. 172). While Hartman (1997) is not insinuating there are no tangible differences between slavery and the postbellum period, she illuminates the ways blackness becomes refigured as an abject category, and pushes back against the "grand narrative of emancipation"

(139). In conceptualizing what I am calling *the afterlife of school segregation*, I also refuse linear narratives of Black educational progress that fail to align with the lived experiences of Black students. I argue that while Black students are no longer subjected to a system of formally segregated schooling, the notion of de facto integration (let alone a liberatory educational experience), remains unrealized.

Similar to the "grand narrative of emancipation" Hartman references, the grand narrative of integration (or even desegregation), remains a central component in the educational trajectory of Black students. Without diminishing the significance of *Brown* and the end of a mandate that very explicitly caste Black students as inferior and forbade their access to the material resources white students received, I wish to think about what the end of formal segregation has meant for Black students who remain (as Black folks did after emancipation), a subjugated group. In exploring the dissonance between de jure and de facto freedom, Hartman notes,

> When those formerly excluded are belatedly conferred with rights and guarantees of equal protection, they have traditionally had difficulty exercising these rights, as long as they are seen as lesser, derivative, or subordinate embodiments of the norm … It is worth examining whether universalism merely dissimulates the stigmatic injuries constitutive of blackness with abstract assertions of equality, sovereignty, and individuality. Indeed, if this is the case, can the dominated be liberated by universalist assertions? (123)

Hence, as Black folk cease in being legal chattel and are (in theory) legally entitled to the same fundamental rights as white citizens, the status of blackness as abjection leads to their inability to enact rights reserved for *real human beings*. Likewise, when considering Black students' belated access to equal rights in education, what does it mean for this population to try to take up these "universal" rights in desegregated educational spaces? Where Hartman questions whether the dominated can be "liberated by universalist assertions," it would behoove us to also question whether Black students en masse may achieve a liberatory educational experience in what we consider to be a system of universal public education.

Without essentializing any one Black educational experience, suffice it to say that numerous scholars have articulated the myriad ways Black students have continually been racialized, dehumanized, hypersexualized, and so forth in schools before, during, and long after desegregation. Even the title of a recent annual Association for the Study of African American Life and History (ASALH) conference was "The Crisis in Black Education," despite the fact that ASALH does not generally focus specifically on Black education. In other words, while it is clear that Black students have made significant advancements in education, there is an increasing sensibility that Black students experience schooling as anti-Black. While a full explication of the afterlife of school segregation is beyond the scope of this current work, I want to begin to elaborate what it means for Black students when schools are "structured by anti-black solidarity" (Wilderson, 2010, p. 58), when antiblackness is endemic to and central to the Black schooling experience (Dumas, 2016; Dumas & ross, 2016).

In some ways, the afterlife of school segregation looks like a white male police officer viciously slamming a Black girl student's head into concrete and dragging her across her South Carolina classroom (Fausset & Southall, 2015) in a way impossible to imagine for example, if one replaced the Black girl with a blonde haired white girl (or a dog for that matter)—doubly impossible if the cop was racialized Black. In some ways the afterlife of segregation looks like a sea of white women teachers arriving to school to teach Black children, brandishing NYPD t-shirts to show their support for the police department who choked Eric Garner to death Radio Rahim style in broad daylight just days earlier (Ryan, 2014). In still other ways, it looks like Black student referrals, suspensions, expulsions, kick outs, and push outs to prison, from toddlers to teens to tweens. It looks like searches and seizures, police dogs and metal detectors, backs against lockers, grips around throats, hands up don't shoot.

While these more explicitly violent examples may be more readily recognized as unjust, the afterlife of school segregation necessitates we also interrogate the routine and reoccurring practices of schooling that cause Black suffering, melancholy, and indignities in schooling. Just as during slavery, where Hartman encourages us to question what it means "that the violence of slavery or the pained existence of the enslaved, if discernible, is only so in the most heinous and grotesque examples and not in the quotidian routines of slavery" (21), the afterlife of school segregation is also about the more quotidian ways Black students suffer in schools. In these ways, the afterlife of school segregation is about Black erasure and misrepresentation in curricular content where for example, Black students may learn that the enslaved were "workers" who came to the U.S. in the context of immigration (Fernandez & Hauser, 2015). It looks like the very notion that students should be provided an accurate assessment of the historical trajectory of this country being pigeon holed as a radical perspective. It looks like diversity initiative after diversity initiative, like being guinea pigs for the latest educational fads (e.g. technology and coding trends, Vakil & Ayers, 2019). It looks like vocational education and military-funded initiatives wrapped in diversity rhetoric. It looks like graduating high school without ever having a Black teacher. It means inadequate and inferior material resources, a lack of access to rigorous classes, or gaining access, only to be marginalized and othered. It means irremediable implicit biases. It means no recess, no arts, no play, no exploration, no noise, no stepping. out. of. line. Test after test after test. Teaching to the test. Learning for the test.

So then, what is the place of blackness in U.S. public education? Where is the place for Black students in U.S. public education? Sexton (2011) posits,

"Black life is not lived in the world that it lives in, but it is lived underground, in outer space" (28). What might the underground, the outer space, look like in the context of education? What would it mean for us to "call a spade a spade" as Du Bois (1935) so simply puts it or to heed Derrick Bell's (1992) call nearly 30 years ago to stop fighting for the unrealistic goal of racial equality and develop "a mechanism to make life bearable in a society where blacks are a permanent subordinate class" (377)? What would it mean to literally and figuratively GET OUT? To "steal away" (Hartman, 1997, p. 66)? Hartman notes, "In effect, by refusing to stay in their place, the emancipated insisted that freedom was a departure, literally and figuratively, from their former condition" (128). What would it mean in the current context to be *on the move?*

## Black Educational Fugitive Space

I utilize the term "fugitive" because I want to suggest that purposefully constructed Black space in education exists in the margin, outside of the auspices of the larger school (though it may be created *within* a larger school). That is, in recognizing that antiblackness is endemic to all aspects of human life (Dumas & ross, 2016), that Black students in education live in the afterlife of school segregation, Black educational fugitive space is born, created, and in direct response to the rampant antiblackness in the larger world, and in U.S. public schools; it may serve as makeshift land, and provide makeshift citizenship to people whose humanity is consistently made impossible on the outside.

I want to offer then, a consideration of fugitive Black space in education as what Christina Sharpe (2016) calls "wake work" (20), or "ways of seeing and imagining responses to terror in the varied and various ways that our Black lives are lived under occupation; ways that attest to the modalities of Black life lived in, as, under, and despite Black death" (20). I want to offer the notion of Black educational fugitive space as search, as destination, as departure, as fugitivity, as the margin, as underground, as undercommons, as outer space, as submarine, as the possibility of "the absolute overturning, the absolute turning of this mutherfucker out" (Moten, 2013, p. 742). In other words, if we conceptualize the Black educational experience as existing within the afterlife of school segregation, where antiblackness precludes Black humanity and inherently positions Black children as uneducable, then the notion of school "reform" for Black children becomes a patronizing insult added to centuries of anti-Black injury. Without diminishing educational policy initiatives that may serve to ameliorate the educational experiences of some Black children, the afterlife of school segregation necessitates we problematize the possibility of educational policies that create liberatory schooling experiences for Black students in an anti-Black world. Hence, if we acknowledge the egregiousness of antiblackness, and the permanence of race demands a permanent move underground, underwater, (outer)space, what then might *Black educational fugitive space* look like? While I resist the inclination toward a Black space cookbook, I want to offer some initial thoughts that might aid us in conceptualizing Black educational fugitive space, and serve as an invitation for further inquiry and collective thought.

Certainly we have, since the social construction of race, engaged in the production of Black space—from what Hartman (1997) describes as "stealing away" when the enslaved would appropriate space in the form of clandestine meetings, to current Black places and spaces in education—both inside and outside of the institution of public schooling. In theorizing Black educational fugitive space, however, I wish to focus on the potentiality (and what I have at times observed in my work as actuality) of a particular kind of Black space in education—what we might conceptualize as homeplace (hooks, 1990), as marginal space (hooks, 1990), where we might gather to *discover and enter* into unlivability (Moten, 2013 pg. 746, italics in original).

Hartman (1997) discusses the ways the enslaved created "social space in which the assertion of needs, desires, and counterclaims could be collectively aired, thereby granting property a social life and an arena or shared identification with other slaves" (69). Similarly, in the afterlife of school segregation, Black students and educators may construct homeplaces in what hooks (1990) describes as "a safe place where Black people could affirm one another and by so doing heal many of the wounds inflicted by racist domination" (42). She continues, "We could not learn to love or respect ourselves in the culture of white supremacy, on the outside; it was there on the *inside*, in that 'homeplace,' most often created and kept by Black women, that we had the opportunity to grow and develop, to nurture out spirits" (42, italics added). When hooks notes the ways folks could "nurture our spirits" denied outside of these homeplaces, she refers to the impossibility of Black humanity in the larger anti–Black society and the ways these homeplaces provided a space "where one could freely confront the issue of humanization, where one could resist" (42). As a part of the impossibility of Black humanity, hooks asserts the unfeasibility of Black self-love within the context of antiblackness; homeplaces then, became spaces where Black folks could reimagine blackness and develop healthy Black subjectivities.

When considering Black educational fugitive space in the context of afterlife of school segregation, we may consider hooks' notion of marginality as we think about Black space as homeplace. Where homeplaces offer a space for resistance, hooks (1990) argues, "Opposition is not enough. In that vacant space after one has resisted, there is still the necessity to become. To make oneself anew" (14). The margin hooks refers to is a

> site of radical possibility, a space of resistance ... a central location for
> the production of a counter-hegemonic discourse that is not just found
> in words ... a site one stays in, clings to even, because it nourishes one's

capacity to resist. It offers one the possibility of a radical perspective from which to see and create, to imagine alternatives, new worlds. (149–150)

I want to suggest that Black educational fugitive space is located in these margins—where yearning and imagining meet and become. Black space fuels itself in the margins and claims "the ground on which we are constructing, 'homeplace'" (19), where Black folks can articulate a politics of refusal, and reimagine themselves in opposition to antiblackness.

Still, hooks (1990) cautions us that there is an important distinction to be made between marginalities imposed by oppressive structures, and the marginalities we choose for ourselves or make our own, "that marginality one chooses as a site of resistance—as location of radical openness and possibility … which gives us a new location to articulate our sense of the world" (153). It is within these margins, that Black educational fugitive space engages in struggling, in reimagining, and in becoming; it engages Black educational futurities, and considers blackness beyond the past and present—it nurtures the political act of Black dreaming. While Black space may be produced in a specific place (Frank's classroom for example), it is not a place in and of itself. Black space is fluid, embodied, and can travel beyond the places in which participants produce it.

While Black educational fugitive space is not limited to this musing, I offer these initial thoughts as an invitation to continue the collective conversation around what it means to conceptualize an educational project for Black students in particular—about what it means to consider the ways we may produce and reproduce spaces that engage the reality of antiblackness and the "possibilities of redress" Hartman, 1997, p. 72). Utilizing the frame of the afterlife of school segregation helps us to step back and consider Black educational fugitive space outside of its potential to interact with the larger public sphere. In other words, when considering various programs in public schools, education scholars often evaluate their usefulness based on the ways they interact with standard measures of academic success (i.e. does the program raise test scores? Does it increase attendance? Does it decrease disciplinary incidents and so forth)? This work encourages us to consider the usefulness of Black space for Black students in anti-Black schools and in an anti-Black world. If we consider this production of space as the political act of constructing homeplace, we are able to consider its usefulness for being a departure, a refuge for Black students who face the impossibility of Black humanity. If we conceptualize Black educational fugitive space as a "radical site of possibility," we must consider the ways this space is generally disallowed, and what it means when we are able to carve it out, to maintain it in schools and in a society that takes a legal and ideological stance against it. While fugitivity may not *yet* mean freedom (Sexton, 2016), as Darius Lovehall so eloquently put it, it's "about the possibility of the thing" (Addis Wechsler Pictures & Witcher, T., 1997).

## References

Addis Wechsler Pictures (Producer), & Witcher, T. (Director). (1997). *Love Jones* [Motion picture]. USA: New Line Cinema.

Bell, D. (1992). Racial realism. *Connecticut Law Review, 24*(2), 363–380.

Dead Prez (2000). They Schools on *Let's Get Free* [Vinyl, LP, Album]. New York, NY: Loud Records.

Delgado, R. (1995). *Critical Race Theory: The Cutting Edge*. Philadelphia, PA: Temple University.

Du Bois, W. B. (1935). Does the Negro need separate schools?. *Journal of Negro Education*, 328–335.

Dumas, M. J. (2016). Against the dark: Antiblackness in education policy and discourse. *Theory Into Practice, 55*(1), 11–19.

Dumas, M. J., & ross, k. m. (2016). "Be Real Black for Me." Imagining BlackCrit in Education. *Urban Education, 51*(4), 415–442.

Fausset, R. & Southall, A. (2015, October 26). Video Shows Officer Flipping Student in South Carolina, Prompting Inquiry. *New York Times*. Retrieved from: www.nytimes.com/2015/10/27/us/officers-classroom-fight-with-student-is- caught-on-video.html?_r=0/.

Fernandez, M. & Hauser, C. (2015, October 5). Texas Mother Teaches Textbook Company a Lesson on Accuracy. *New York Times*. Retrieved from: https://www.nytimes.com/2015/10/06/us/publisher-promises-revisions-aftertextbook-refers-to-african-slaves-as-workers.html/.

Hartman, S. (1997). *Scenes of Subjection*. New York: Oxford University Press.

Hartman, S. V. (2007). *Lose Your Mother: A Journey Along the Atlantic Slave Route*. New York: Farrar, Straus and Giroux

Hartman, S. V., & Wilderson, F. B. (2003). The position of the unthought. *Qui Parle, 13*(2), 183–201.

hooks, b. (1990). *Yearning: Race, Gender, and Cultural Politics* (p. 57). Boston: South End Press.

Moten, F. (2013). Blackness and nothingness (mysticism in the flesh). *South Atlantic Quarterly, 112*(4), 737–780.

Ryan, E.G. (2014, September 5). NYC Teachers Wear Shirts to Support Cops after Cop Murders Black Man. Jezzebel. Retrieved from: http://jezebel.com/nyc-teachers- wear-shirts-to-support-cops-after-cop-murd-1631002384.

Sexton, J. (2011). The social life of social death: On Afro-pessimism and Black optimism. *InTensions, 5*(1).

Sexton, J. (2016). Afro-pessimism: The unclear word. *Rhizomes: Cultural Studies in Emerging Knowledge, 29*.

Sharpe, C. (2016). *In the Wake: On blackness and Being*. Durham, NC: Duke University Press.

Vakil, S. & Ayers, R. (2019). The racial politics of STEM education in the USA: Interrogations and explorations. *Race Ethnicity and Education, 22*(4), 449–458.

Wilderson III, F. B. (2010). *Red, White & Black: Cinema and the Structure of US Antagonisms*. Durham, NC: Duke University Press.

Wilderson III, F. B. (2015). Untitled [lecture].

# 6

# ANTI-BLACKNESS IS EQUILIBRIUM

## How "Disparity" Logics Pathologize Black Male Bodies and Render Other Black Bodies Invisible

*Hari Ziyad and Timothy DuWhite*

## Introduction

In response to the far more severe punitive actions facing Black students as opposed to their white counterparts, the parents, teachers, and advocates of Black pupils often proclaim there to be a racial "double-standard"[1] in school discipline that must be addressed. However, to make such a claim is to erase the standard of anti-Blackness that has long been set by the history of this world. To regulate disparities in school discipline to such a simple term is to ignore the economic, social, and political benefits civil society enjoys *solely* off the backs of Black people who are punished by the carceral systems which are foundational to school discipline. Put another way, were it not for Black suffering such as that which is caused by anti-Black disciplinary actions, there would be no privileges for white students to afford in contrast—privileges this society relies upon. As Saidiya Hartman explains, in the afterlife of slavery "skewed life chances, limited access to health and education, premature death, incarceration, and impoverishment"[2] are the rules of the game. If "slavery is a relational dynamic"[3] as Frank B. Wilderson III posits, these rules cannot be expected to cease to have effect simply because the players are shifted around. When the standard of anti-Blackness persists, the relationship between the Slave (Black) and the Human (non-Black) requires "double-standards" for white and Black student discipline, because it demands Black social death in order for others in society to lay claim to human life they hold so dear.

The problems with seeking to "address" such disparities without addressing the anti-Blackness underlying them go beyond simple futility. Disparity logics which assume "double-standards" can be simply "addressed" rely upon the false idea that Black students are afforded the same subjecthood as non-Black students, and thus these logics fall victim to the problematics of the "language of freedom" as described by Hartman: "… Once you realize it's limits and be-gin to see its inexorable investment in certain notions of subject and subjection, then that language of freedom no longer becomes that which rescues the slave from his or her former condition, but the site of the re-elaboration of that con-dition, rather than its transformation."[4]

We see this re-elaboration of the condition of Black student suffering in many of the efforts to curtail suspension rates across the country. In Fresno, California, the County Office of Education has decided to address what has been made clear to be a racialized problem of suspensions by adopting the Pos-itive Behavioral Interventions and Supports (PBIS) model established by the U.S. Department of Education, which "helps schools establish clear behavioral and social expectations in a system that supports all students, acknowledges positive behavior, promotes academic learning and reduces the number of dis-cipline referrals and suspensions on a campus," according to Fresno County Superintendent of Schools, Jim A. Yovino.[5]

Yet the anti-Black rules of the game—Black suffering—remain in place, and so this new model is also rife with unaltered anti-Black carceral logics. As reported by journalist Mackenzie Mays for *The Fresno Bee*, PBIS offers offenders

> a chance to avoid out-of-school punishment by attending a sort of mock court, where they can apologize and hear the victim's side of the story. Students' families are invited to attend, and if a victim doesn't want to participate, volunteers will represent a 'victim panel' so the process can continue. An offender typically leaves with a meaningful consequence related to the offense that doesn't force them out of school.[6]

Relying on a "mock court" modeled after the very judicial system that impris-ons and murders Black people at devastating rates,[7] PBIS does not deter Black students' paths into the carceral system, but rather further normalizes and pre-pares them for it. Terms like "meaningful consequence" in this context only help to reinforce the plausibility we are taught to unquestionably offer all law enforcement and their verdicts on Black lives. This is an example of how an intervention that Monique W. Morris explains in *Pushout: The Criminalization of Black Girls in School*, "might miss the oppressive condition—present in insti-tutions and in society at large—that place [them] in harm's way."[8]

Similarly, the Miami-Dade County Public Schools system has been her-alded[9] as a national example of how to address exclusionary and punitive dis-cipline after they claimed to have "eliminated" out-of-school suspensions. But a new report by the Advancement Project illuminates how many of these same students who had previously been suspended are now simply being sent home without a record of their suspension. Further, the district's Lockout Policy bars students from their classes for an entire period when they arrive late, punishing students by keeping them out of the classroom in much the same way a suspension would. Finally, the district's "alternative" to out-of-school suspensions, Success Centers, were found to generally be places where students are warehoused without appropriate instruction, just as they would be were they suspended.[10] This is what "addressing" anti-Black "double standards" in school without addressing anti-Blackness looks like.

Unless anti-Blackness as *the relationship between Blackness and society* is reckoned with, all advocacy for Black students will continue to re-elaborate and obscure the problems facing Black students, including and especially advocacy based on gender.

## Disparity Logics and the Re-Elaboration of Anti-Black Gendered Violence

These same disparity logics that fail to account for anti-Blackness are behind many of the gendered "solutions" to the challenges faced by Black boys and male students, responses which thereby also re-elaborate and continue to ultimately harm *all* Black students. As illuminated by Michael Dumas and Joseph Derrick Nelson, "black boyhood itself has been rendered both unimagined and unimaginable," as anti-Blackness collapses Black boyhood into Black manhood and Black manhood into a conception of a violent and inherent delinquency. Dumas and Nelson argue that this visibility of Black male delinquency, but not of Black boyhood, has resulted in

> ample federal and state interest in and funding for Black (and Latino) male interventions (e.g., the Obama administration's My Brother's Keeper initiative), (while) there is a troubling lack of support for research and programs related to the educational lives and struggles of girls of color ... even as the data show that Black girls and many other girls of color lag far behind white girls in access to social and educational opportunities.[11]

Gendered disparity logics that do not account for anti-Blackness recognize the problems facing Black boys, but only to paint them as either uniquely targeted or uniquely uneducable men. At the same time, these logics ignore the problems facing Black girls, trans, or gender non-conforming children and adults altogether, essentially invisibilizing them and the resources they might require. In either case, anti-Black violences—the rules of the game—remain in place yet again, harming Black people of all (non-)genders. By relying on gender disparity logics without accounting for anti-Blackness, we re-elaborate anti-Black violence across and beyond the gender spectrum, while concealing it under the guise of male hypercriminality and non-male hyperinvisibility.

This obscuring of anti–Blackness by the use of gendered disparity logics can also be witnessed in the prevailing conversations around police violence. As Wilderson explains:

> The violence against Black people which we are witnessing on YouTube, Instagram, and TV news is conveniently gendered as violence against Black men. But there is a problem here, and it is twofold: we tend to lose sight of the fact Black women, children and LGBT people are losing their breath through the technologies of social death, just as Black hetero men are, albeit in less visible and less mediatised ways; we also get drawn into responding to the phobic anxieties of White and non-Black civil society, the threat of the Black man; and as such we offer sustenance to that juggernaut of civil society even as we try to dismantle it.[12]

As Wilderson highlights, when anti–Blackness persists, visibility of what is recognized as the problems *facing* a segment of Black people easily turns into the problem *of* that segment. Just as some Black men attempt to use the very real staggering rates of Black men in fatal conflict with the police to support narratives of Black men as some *especial* victim of anti–Blackness, others use these rates to support their fantasies of Black men as violent threats. All the while, Black non-men experience constant deaths both material and social, sometimes intra-communally at the hands of Black cisgender heterosexual men, that continually go ignored. By falling for the ruse of a gender disparity logic that does not account for an underlying anti–Blackness, all Black people continue to suffer.

## Gendered Violence, Unelaborated

The failure of disparity logics should be an important consideration for how we seek to utilize humanistic feminist and queer interventions in the work we claim to be doing for Black students and children. As Calvin Warren states, Black students have a "different relationship to violence" than non–Black subjects, queer and female, because they have a "different relationship to 'nothingness.'"[13] The tempting response to the failures of Black cisgender heterosexual men to recognize the limits of positioning themselves as *especial* victims of anti–Blackness is to reverse this conceptualization, and position female, queer, and/or trans Black people as having it "worse than" others within a hierarchical matrix Black suffering. We are arguing that Black people's unique relationship to "nothingness" as required by our lack of human subjecthood means that there is no matrix. Black suffering exists outside of the realm of human comparison, and therefore cannot be understood within a human hierarchy of violence, especially given the un-imaginability of Black childhood.

As Kevin Rigby, Jr. pointed out in a private conversation, the importance of understanding Black people's relationship to nothingness within the context of gendered violence was illuminated by the recent story of a murdered 17-year-old transgender Athens, Ohio girl named Ava Le'Ray Barrin—or at least by the way certain progressive media outlets reported on this story. As was repeated in numerous articles, Barrin was the fourteenth trans person to be violently killed in 2017 (according to the Human Rights Campaign),[14] and, as these articles emphasized, her death was certainly indicative of the profound extent of the crisis that is violence against Black trans women. However, in a rush to confirm the narrative already laid out for us by disparity logics—a rush born largely out of the desire to prove a "worse than" position within a hierarchy of violence for trans women, her murderer, Jalen Breon Brown, was quickly described as a cisgender Black man, when in fact Brown was a member of a rival transgender group that was feuding with Barrin's.[15]

The oversimplification of these types of narratives—caused by the refusal to account for anti-Blackness—prevent them from lending themselves to any solution. By conforming Barrin's story to the disparity model as laid out, she more easily becomes a number (fourteenth trans woman) and hashtag, and the threat is more easily diverted from the anti-Black violence which puts Black trans women into harm's way in the first place to the criminally delinquent Black man (almost every article in question contained nothing more than bare-bones information confirming these three points). In this way, Barrin becomes invisibilized once again, and her killer is misgendered in the same way and with the same quickness as what those calling for Brown's head would have been up in arms for if Brown was the one who was killed. Ignoring the underlying anti-Blackness—the relationship between Blackness and nothingness (the "Outside"[16] of human subjectivity) that turns hierarchies of violence into re-elaborations of anti-Black conditions—disallows the necessary individuality of Barrin's story in order to more easily conform to the language of disparity logics that require hierarchies of violence.

Similarly, this desire to allocate Black people's experiences with violence into a neatly delineated hierarchy of violence without accounting for anti-Blackness invisiblizes the crucial realities of Black gender non-conforming people. In an effort to keep disparity logics in place, the lived experiences of members of the Black gender non-conforming community are often conflated with the experiences of others. As illuminated by the case of Kenneth Bostick, who was widely regarded as "the tenth transgender murder" in 2017, a designation that forced his friends and family members to come out and clarify that Kenneth used he/him pronouns despite being non-conforming,[17] violence against gender non-conforming people who are not trans is very much a reality too, a reality that we are ill-equipped to reckon with if we are following anti-Black binaristic gendered scripts (interestingly, various publications alternated between calling

Bosnick a transgender man and a transgender woman). Much of the violence we see being inflicted upon Black transgender women is due to their gender being read or determined illegitimate—it doesn't *conform* neatly into the standard of human femininity. However, in attempting to normalize a space for Black transgender people along the gender binary, which is a function of the disparity logics we are critiquing in this piece, gender non-conforming people become proof of yet another re-elaboration of the problem.

This is not to say that intra-communal violence isn't real, nor that certain expressions of it aren't more commonly wielded against certain margins of the Black community. Even given a relationship with nothingness—even within this realm "Outside" of human subjectivity—Black people have individualized experiences which are gendered in important ways, and this cannot be ignored. But, as Wilderson points out,

> we come to think of our oppression as being *essentially* gendered, as opposed to being gendered in important ways. This, I believe, gives us a false sense of agency; a sense that we can redress the violence of social death in ways which are analogous to the tactics of our so-called allies of colour. We *want* the violence against us to have a gendered integrity, in the way that it does when it is levied against the subaltern.

This sense of false agency contributes to forgetting to implicate the anti-Black state that pre-emptively renders Black life aberrant, and therefore violence against it always logical, when discussing anti-Black violence being inflicted both upon and by Black people. But it is the state which first consigns Blackness to inhumanity, across our multiplicity of gender expressions. We are gendered in important ways, but we are *essentially* left out of recognition of humanity.

In order to properly address the problems facing Black students, we argue that Blackness has its own gendered integrity, one that can wrestle with questions of Black queerness, woman-ness, and transness, and the specificity of intra-communal violence against those positions outside of humanistic disparity logics that alternatively erase and criminalize Black children. This is the unique gendered integrity Marquis Bey touches upon in *The Trans*-ness of Blackness, the Blackness of Trans*-ness*. Bey builds off of the work of Hortense Spillers to argue:

> Blackness rests in the in-between, and this 'between' is also a movement of flight, of escape, of fugitivity from the confines of ontological pinning down. The pinning down requires fixation and definable locations, but as in-between, blackness is that elusive interstitiality; it is that 'posture of critical insurgency' ... Excessive of the logic of sovereignty—governability, logic qua logic—is blackness, and it is always smoldering, fissuring, crackling.[18]

By contrast, anti-Blackness is equilibrium. It is the fixedness, the balance of violence, that Blackness resists. It is the state, the schools, and their disciplinary systems. It is the way Black people too often fall back into disciplining one another, essentializing other Black people into one-dimensional representations of our gendered possibilities. It is the gender binary. And in resisting anti-Blackness, we must ask: How do we reimagine gender in a way that allows *all* Black children room to define their social and material lives? How do we refuse the pressures to hypercriminalize or hyperinvisibilize Black children before they have even started along this journey? How do we recognize the uniqueness of their journeys, and acknowledge how this uniqueness is gendered, without projecting anti-Black limits onto them? If we are ever to truly address the problems facing Black students, these questions are a good place to start.

## Notes

1  Sablich, Liz. "7 Findings that Illustrate Racial Disparities in Education | Brookings Institution." Brookings. Brookings, July 29, 2016.
2  Hartman, Saidiya V. *Lose Your Mother: A Journey along the Atlantic Slave Route.* New York: Farrar, Straus and Giroux, 2008. p. 6.
3  Wilderson, Frank B. "Afro-Pessimism & the End of Redemption." *The Occupied Times*, 12 Sep. 2016, theoccupiedtimes.org/?p=14236.
4  Hartman, Saidiya V., and Frank B. Wilderson III. "The Position of the Unthought." *Qui Parle*, vol. 13, no. 2, 2003, p. 185. doi:10.1215/quiparle.13.2.
5  Yovino, Jim A. "FCOE Recognizes 102 Schools for Improving, Reducing Suspensions." Fresno County Superintendent of Schools. fcoe.org/news/spotlight/fcoe-recognizes-102-schools-improving-reducing-suspensions.
6  Mays, Mackenzie. "As Expulsions, Suspensions Decrease at Fresno Schools, Concerns about out-of-Control Classrooms Grow." *The Fresno Bee*, Dec. 16, 2015. www.fresnobee.com/news/local/education/eye-on-education/article49482150.html.
7  Nellis, Ashley. "The Color of Justice: Racial and Ethnic Disparity in State Prisons." The Sentencing Project. www.sentencingproject.org/publications/color-of-justice-racial-and-ethnic-disparity-in-state-prisons/.
8  Morris, Monique W. *Pushout: The Criminalization of Black Girls in School.* New York: The New Press, 2016, p. 225.
9  O'Connor, John. "Miami-Dade Schools Eliminating Out-Of-School Suspensions." *Statement Impact*, NPR, July 29, 2005. stateimpact.npr.org/florida/2015/07/29/miami-dade-schools-eliminating-out-of-school-suspensions/.
10  Power U Center for Social Change & The Advancement Project. "Miami-Dade County Public Schools: The Hidden Truth." *The Advancement Project.* Sep. 6, 2017, p. 26.
11  Dumas, Michael and Joseph Derrick Nelson. "(Re)Imagining Black Boyhood: Toward a Critical Framework for Educational Research." *Harvard Educational Review*, vol. 86, no. 1, p. 30.
12  Wilderson 2016.
13  Calvin Warren, "Onticide: Toward an Afro-Pessimistic Queer Theory" (printout of presentation, Annual Meeting of the American Studies Association, Washington, D.C., November 21–24, 2013), p. 9.

14 Campaign, Human Rights. "Violence Against the Transgender Community in 2017." *Human Rights Campaign*, HRC, www.hrc.org/resources/violence-against-the-transgender-community-in-2017.

15 Johnson, Joe. "Athens Teen's Shooting Death Linked to Feud between Transgender Groups, Police Say." *Online Athens*, Online Athens, 28 June 2017, onlineathens.com/local-news/2017-06-28/athens-teen-s-shooting-death-linked-feud-between-transgender-groups-police-say.

16 A term I played with in a previous piece: Ziyad, Hari. "Playing 'Outside' in the Dark Blackness in a Postwhite World." *Critical Ethnic Studies Association*. 3.1. 2017.

17 Editors, NewNowNext. "We Got It Wrong." *LOGO News*, LOGO, 8 May 2017, www.newnownext.com/brenda-bostick-trans-woman-murder/05/2017/.

18 Bey, Marquis. "The Trans*-ness of Blackness, the Blackness of Trans*-ness." *TSQ: Transgender Studies Quarterly*. 4.9. 2017. pp. 279.

# PART II
# Conceptual Considerations

# 7

# RADICAL HOPE, EDUCATION AND HUMANITY

*Carl A. Grant*

In framing this chapter, I bring together two statements that I see as parallel in accuracy and explanatory power in speaking truth about America. The first is Douglass' and Wilderson's (Douglass & Wilderson, 2013) assertion that from slavery to the present "a black man is being beaten" is the archetypal scene that haunts American life. The second is Thurgood Marshall's statement, "Racism separates, but it never liberates." Both observations' honesty about the failure of American democracy speak to darkness and suffering; the ontological absence of Blacks in the glories and everydayness of "We the people" and the denial of Black people full participation in US civil society because of the color of their skin. Although, for almost 400 years, African Americans have had to deal with social and political death and the negation of their humanity, they had maintained hope—a belief in themselves both as individuals and as a collective since 1619, when they first arrived in the US enslaved.

As a concept, hope has been a focus of discussion throughout history, and across academic disciplines (e.g., psychology, history). I turn to political philosophy (Rorty, 2000; Bloch, 1938), American pragmatism, in general (e.g., Dewey 2012; James, 1896), but specifically, African American pragmatism (e.g., Du Bois, 1903; Locke, 1925; West, 1989; Claude, 2007) to theorize *radical hope* for this chapter. In so doing, I discuss how African Americans understand education as a space of *radical hope*, and the role of *radical hope* within pathways on the journey toward Black freedom and the acceptance of the humanity of Black people.

## "Radical Hope"

"Radical Hope is the ability to maintain hope in a meaningful existence even when one's existence has lost all meaning. It is hope that goes beyond one's ability to formulate an idea of what one hopes for" (Furrow, 2007, p. 2). Solnit (2016) argues, radical hope is the idea that what people do has consequences, even though how and when the consequences will matter, and who and what they may impact is not known beforehand. *Radical hope* has structure; among its elements are rationality, education, history, and persistence. It has cognitive resolve, encourages planned collective action, is receptive of political efficacy, and is support by courage and "collective excellence." It is more than optimism and resists pessimism (Bloch, 1938; Lear, 2006). I discovered the phrase "radical hope" as the title on the cover of Jonathan Lear's (2008) book: *Radical Hope: Ethics in the Face of Cultural Devastation.* Later, I saw it again in the titles of De Robertis' (2016) and Pearson's (2011) books. Lear's book is a story of the last great chief of the Crow nation, Plenty Coups, reflecting on the devastation of the Crow's civilization in Montana. Lear's (2008) *Radical Hope* addresses how a people stripped of their way of life imagine how to survive and then venture forth to thrive again. *Radical hope,* as Lear discusses, came to be because of the cultural devastation of the Crow Civilization by American imperialism. When the Crow people's land was taken by the Federal Government, they were moved to a reservation. Living on the reservation meant the Crow had to give up their way of life, which included carrying out of traditional rituals in the places of their ancestors. As Chief, Plenty Coups was confronted with how he and his people should live with the buffalo gone, the hearts of his people emotionally and spiritually ruined, and their ability to lift themselves up destroyed.

Lear, a philosopher and psychoanalyst, discusses how Plenty Coups deals with the devastation of Crow traditions and narratives with their life meaning gone. Instead of plunging deeper into the darkness and giving way to social, political and human vulnerability, Plenty Coups senses a spark, *radical hope* born out of the suffering and mourning. Lear (2008) explains, although the Crows have had their telos destroyed, their moral reasoning holds firm, supported by the core of their tradition, that enabled the development of courage and clarity at such a catastrophic moment. Plenty Coups believed that as the Crows faced the future, in time, they would develop new rituals and narratives that have meaning for them, though probably not the way they could now imagine. Lear (2008) argues Plenty Coups' actions signified a radical and courageous stance of hope in the face of anxiety and uncertainty.

I have always been interested in the "hope" (and suffering) of Black people, since my preteen years when I first read about the kidnapping, Middle Passage, hush harbors during enslavement, and Fredrick Douglass' and other enslaved Blacks' fight to become literate. During this period of self-teaching, I always searched for that hope I believed was embodied within Black people, based upon what I knew about being Black and living Black in solidarity with other Blacks in Bronzeville, Chicago, where I grew up. I read of "hope"—such as Du Bois' (1903) *aspirational hope* for Blacks with his research and publication of the *Philadelphia Negro* and the *substantive hope* of the 1960s Civil Rights

Movement—and, I believed that hope was in the DNA of Black people. Now, in this chapter, I want to think about education as a space of radical hope—that is hope that develops out of suffering and mourning, the destruction of a way life in the face of anxiety and uncertainty—and the role of radical hope in the struggle for freedom and the acceptance and appreciation of Black humanity.

I borrow from Lear's (2008) discussion of radical hope, keeping in mind that "a way of life had come to an end" (Lear, 2008, p. 9) for Black people when they were kidnaped and enslaved and ironically a "way of life came to an end" for Blacks when Emancipation freed them from enslavement; and again, after Reconstruction, when they had to live under institutionalized segregation and Jim and Jane Crow laws. The attention that Lear (2008) gives to how radical hope came to be, the concepts of courage, human vulnerability, resiliency, and ways of living, among others, were useful to this chapter. Also, my reading of other books and articles allowed me to shape and structure radical hope for my use.

## Education and Humanity

Black people strove toward learning letters (education) in the hush harbors of slave quarters and from stolen glances at words on printed pages. Self-teaching was a form of protest, resistance, and hope (Williams, 2007). Education was enslaved, segregated, and so-called freed Black people's spark of radical hope as they struggled against social and political death (Sexton, 2011). Below, I provide two examples of how African Americans understood education as a space of *radical hope*, and the role of *radical hope* within pathways on the journey toward Black freedom and the acceptance of the humanity of Black people. The first example is set during enslavement in the US; however, it begins with the Kidnapping—the cultural devastation of the lives of 12.5 million Africans, of which 10.7 million survived the horrors of the Middle Passage to land in North and South America and the Caribbean (Gates, 2014). According to Gates (2014), 388,000 of the Africans kidnapped survived the Atlanta crossing to arrive in the US. In the US they were sold as property, placed in a slave coffle, and moved (often walking for days) to their owner's home where they served as the work force that made America the preeminent economic, military, and social power.

Enslaved Blacks, stripped of how they had lived for years, including the loss of family, friends, culture, traditions, and narratives had to imagine how to survive and then venture forth to thrive again. Education became enslaved Blacks' space of radical hope, in that it was through literacy that enslaved Blacks believed they could secure freedom; and with freedom, they could develop new traditions, narratives, and rituals, and show the beauty, uniqueness and complexity of their humanity. Williams (2005) states, "Access to the written word, whether scriptural or political, revealed a world beyond bondage in which African Americans could image themselves free to think and behave as they chose" (p. 7). For many enslaved Blacks, acquiring reading and writing skills meant freedom—if not physical freedom, then intellectual freedom (Williams, 2005). Black people understood the path to freedom would be filled with struggles and they looked upon struggles against white doctrine and domination as a way to make living as an enslaved person bearable. Enslaved Blacks saw literacy—learning to read, do math, and to write—as resistance, in that it undermined white authority and caused whites to become concerned about their ability to control their "property." Mental activities such as being curious, eavesdropping, and memorizing indicated that Blacks were intelligent and would offer counternarratives to the lies and myths of humanitarianism told about enslavement.

Owners of enslaved Blacks were aware that knowledge was power and that control of enslaved people could not be based solely on physical coercion. Therefore, slave codes were established making it illegal to teach slaves to read or write. Both Black and white people believed literacy would bring down slavery. An enslaved Black who had learned to write could write passes that would allow him/her and others to escape North or to Canada. Antiliteracy laws included fines, whippings, and, imprisonment for teaching enslaved Blacks to read and write. And antiliteracy laws stated that enslaved Black could be severely punished, including receiving beating and amputation of fingers and toes. Despite the possibility of bodily mutilation and other physical punishment, enslaved Blacks saw education as a spark of radical hope and proceeded to become literate and to develop knew traditions and rituals to take the place of the ones they lost when they were stolen from Africa. Slave narratives became a powerful American genre in literature, offering a counternarrative to the benevolence of slavery; and slave narratives established a tradition of Black women giving voice to the voiceless. Many slave narratives were written by women whose stories told of sexual exploitation and forced separation from their children (e.g., Jacobs, 2000). Black women's stories addressed a genre within slave narratives that Toni Morrison (2015) would speak to years later when she said: "If there is a book you really want to read, but it hasn't been written yet, then you must write it" (p. 1). Education, for enslaved Blacks, because they wanted it and fought to get it, after cultural devastation, suffering and mourning; and they create something, new with it (e.g., narratives, traditions, music, art) made it (education) a space of radical hope.

My second example moves from Enslavement to Emancipation and then to Reconstruction and rise of Black social and political life. This (Reconstruction) important, moment in American history was followed by the destruction or death of Black social and political life as well as many physical deaths (e.g., lynching). No longer enslaved, after 1865, clandestine schools: learning sites in the hush harbors or in a corner in the slave quarters late at night became central features of Emancipation. Blacks, who had learned to read, write, and do math, opened schools for their Black brothers and sisters. In Georgia, for example, freed slaves immediately demanded schooling and attendance at schools over-flowed within a year. The belief about education being a space of radical hope heard and observed during enslavement was realized during Reconstruction. Freed fathers, mothers, and their children looked upon education as the path to freedom and the path that would lead to the acceptance of their humanity.

Scholars (e.g., Bailey, 1995; Franklin, 1994) have identified more than 2,000 African Americans ably serving as officer holders during Reconstruction, demonstrating that Blacks had the knowledge and skills to shape the political, economic, and social life of the South; and debunking the lies about Black in-competence during Reconstruction. The rise of Black families, Black churches, and education took place during Reconstruction.

However, the rise of Black humanity, including the active participation of Blacks in social and political civic affairs angered whites and inspired their hostility. Angry and frustrated that former enslaved Blacks were being allowed to vote, govern, and carry-on as white people do, caused whites to resort to intimidation and violence. Whites formed the Ku Klux Klan, established Black Codes, and institutionalized Jane and Jim Crow segregationist policies to pro-mote white supremacy and maintain white privilege. In twelve years (1865–1877), Reconstruction came to a halt. After little more than a decade, Blacks in the South experienced a form of culture devastation. Blacks were stripped of a way of life that had promise after enslavement and experienced devastation to their cultural and civil existence.

Being emancipated and socially and politically enslaved again, along with having their blackness humiliated, didn't cause Blacks (collectively) to engage in suicidal despair, become indifferent and to stop hoping and striving for a bet-ter way of life. With antiblackness surrounding them, Blacks migrated North, putting the enslaved and the de jure segregated life behind them. City side-walks welcomed them, although often harshly, but education—through at-tending school—continued to be their spark of *radical hope* for acquiring good paying jobs, living the good life they always imagined, and having their chil-dren live even a better life.

Blacks, who had come North in prior decades and were living under de facto segregation, used their collected education (doctors, lawyers, entrepre-neurs) as a space of radical hope to carry out the development of Bronzeville, Harlem, and other spaces that allowed them to live their daily life in a com-munity and as a community without the constant gaze of whites, and for them to express their humanity in art, music, literature, architecture, and living life.

That the Black man is still being beaten (R.L., 2013) in 2017 and racism continues to separate in 2017 is a non-debatable fact. The radical hope that Black people have in education and the role of hope in the struggle for freedom and acquiring the appreciation of Black humanity remains firm today with many Black people. That Black people continue to engage in a tough on-going struggle to have their humanity accepted and appreciated equal to white humanity is a truth. A truth and struggle that some Blacks believe will not end favorably for Blacks. Antiblackness is structurally imbedded, and white power and privilege abounds everywhere.

Whereas I see antiblackness structurally imbedded throughout society, along with white power and privilege, and I do agree with those who argue that for Black humanity to be accepted equally to white humanity, the world as we know it will have to change. That said, I have hope that the world as we know it (racism, white privilege and power) will change, for the world is in crisis, as whiteness struggles to maintain the dominance and privilege of past generation. White dominance and privilege I believe is gradually collapsing and will continue to collapse, this moment of Trump notwithstanding, even as it reinvents itself in different forms. Many Black people continue to have hope in their collected effort and resiliency even when beset by dominating forces. The hope they have is not false hope. It is the radical hope they have in education, their children and grandchildren and other Black children that enables them to believe African Americans will continue to develop new narratives and traditions, and will come to see their humanity accepted and appreciated equal to any other humanity.

## References

Bailey, R. (1995). *Neither Carpetbaggers nor Scalawags: Black Officeholders during the Reconstruction of Alabama, 1867–1878*. Montgomery, AL: Bailey.

Bloch, E. (1938). *The Principle of Hope*. Cambridge, MA: MIT Press.

Claude, E. S. (2007). *In a Shade of Blue: Pragmatism and the Politics of Black America*. Chicago: University of Chicago Press.

*Constitutional Rights Foundation*. (n.d.) Slavery in the American South. www.crf-usa. org/black-history-month/slavery-in-the-american-south.

De Robertis, C. (Ed.). (2016). *Radical Hope: Letters of Love and Dissent in Dangerous Times*. New York: Vintage.

Dewey, J. (2012). *Democracy and Education*. New York: Simon & Schuster.

Douglas, F. (n.d.) Learning to read and write. http://learningabe.info/fd_ ReadandWrite.pdf.

Douglass, P., & Wilderson, F. (2013). The violence of presence: Metaphysics in a blackened world. *The Black Scholar, 43*(4), 117–123.

Du Bois, W. E. B. (1903). *The Souls of Black Folk*. New York: Dover Publications.

Franklin, J. H. (1994). *Reconstruction after the Civil War*. Chicago: University of Chicago Press.

Furrow, D. & Furrow, L. (2007). Radical Hope and the Atheist's Dilemma. *Philosophy on the Mesa*. https://philosophyonthemesa.com/2007/06/21/radical-hope-and-the-atheists-dilemma/.

Gates, H. L. (2014). How many slaves landed in the US? *The Root*. www.theroot.com/ how-many-slaves-landed-in-the-us-1790873989.

Jacobs, H. (2000). *Incidents in the Life of a Slave Girl*. New York: Penguin.

James, W. (1896). The will to believe. *The New World*. https://www.mnsu.edu/philosophy/THEWILLTOBELIEVEbyJames.pdf.

L., R. (2013). Wanderings for the Slave: Black Life and Social Death. *Mute*. www.metamute.org/editorial/articles/wanderings-slave-black-life-and-social-death#sdfootnote3sym.

Lear, J. (2006). *Radica Hope: Ethics in the Face of Cultural Devastation*. Cambridge, MA: Harvard University Press.

Locke, A. (1925). *The New Negro: An Interpretation*. New York. Simon & Schuster.

Morrison, T. (2015). Quoted in Gradient Lair. www.gradientlair.com/.

Pearson, N. (2011). *Radical Hope: Education Equality in Australia*. Collingwood, Australia: Griffin.

Rorty, R. (2000). *Philosophy and Social Hope*. London: Penguin.

Sexton, J. (2011). The social life of social death: On Afro-Pessimism and Black Optimism. *InTensions*, 5(1).

Solnit, R. (2016). *Hope in the Dark: Untold Histories, Wild Possibilities*. Chicago: Haymarket Books.

West, C. (1989). *The American Evasion of Philosophy: A Genealogy of Pragmatism*. Madison, WI: University of Wisconsin Press.

William, H. A. (2007). *Self-Taught: African American Education in Slavery and Freedom*. Chapel Hill, NC: University North Carolina Press.

# 8

# ANTI-BLACKNESS AND THE SCHOOL CURRICULUM

*Keffrelyn D. Brown and Anthony L. Brown*

## Introduction

This chapter draws from the notion of anti–Black racism as a pervasive and mutable construct in U.S. society. As scholars have noted, anti–Black racism helps to advance ideas about Black people as sub-human (Brown, 2018). This troubling construction bears witness to the legacy of dehumanizing knowledge that has followed and been linked to Blackness. This knowledge serves as a backdrop to the suffering that Black people have experienced as travelers in a societal context marred by anti–Black racism. We argue that one of strongest promoters of historically defined anti–Black racism is the American school curriculum. Contingent on the historical context of which race and racism was organized in U.S. society; school curriculum has taken a very specific role in advancing anti–Black racism.

## Theoretical Framework

The theoretical tenets of Black critical theory or *Blackcrit* inform this chapter. Coined by Dumas and ross (2016), this theory argues that in order to examine race in the context of Black people living in the U.S., attention must be given to both racism *and* the specificity of Black life as experienced in a racist society. Key to this framework is attending to the life conditions of Black people, not as a general race project (Omi & Winant, 2014) for understanding racism, but to explicate the specificity of Black suffering as an effect of anti–Black racism. In this chapter, we discuss two key tenets within Black critical theory for understanding how anti-Blackness manifests in school curriculum.

The first is that the construct of Blackness—as sub-human and deviant—coupled with practices of institutional racism are indelible aspects of American society. Here, racism against Black people is not conceptualized as an aberration from an ideal construct of American democracy. Black critical theorists draw attention to the ideas of anti-Blackness to show how they are woven into a narrative of American progress. For example, as the U.S. developed into a stronger sociopolitical and economic democracy, its beginnings were marked by a virulent racism linked to Black life (Bell, 1976). This continues into the present, with anti-Black racism operating as a foundational construct. Black suffering is not a breach from the social contract that defined democracy. Rather, African American oppression is a natural outcome of what Charles Mills (1997) calls the racial contract. The racial contract is the belief that Black inequities are a natural outcome of American society. As a result, racism has a constant presence in social life that adapts and shifts in alignment with the contingencies of history, technology, and political interests. In this chapter, we recognize anti-Blackness, or anti-Black racism as a shifting construct. Racism, then, has taken on different forms as mediated by the conditions of time and space. Frank Wilderson's (2010) words here are useful:

> [T]he structural, or absolute violence, what Loïc Wacquant calls the "carceral continuum," is not a Black experience but a condition of "Black life." It remains constant, paradigmatically, despite changes in its "performance" over time—slave ship, Middle Passage, Slave estate, Jim Crow, the ghetto or prison industrial complex. (p. 75)

Although the contexts of history helped to create different conditions of Black exclusion and suffering, Black life remained enclosed within an ideology of racial exclusion. These forms of anti-Black racism are not just relegated to one space. The construct of race and the practices of racism are all-encompassing in multiple facets of society—including economics, law, philosophy, morality, beauty, and schooling. This conception of power suggests that the dispersal of hegemony is not top-down but is informed by a confluence of discourses and ideological practices.

The second tenet of Black critical theory we draw from in this chapter is the idea that African Americans have consistently fought, challenged, and sought to redefine the discursive and material realities of Black life. We share in the ideas of Afropessimists and critical race theorists that despite the enduring realities of anti-Black racism, African Americans have consisted created and defined an "outer space" (Sexton, 2011) to mitigate the blows of white racism. These spaces, often outside of formal school spaces, are designed to buffer against the epistemic violence incurred by Black students in schools that devalue both their knowledge and personhood (Mills, 1998). In the sections that follow we consider how school curriculum used race to discursively position Black people as the proverbial racial Other.

## Anti-Black Racism is an Enduring and Shifting Construct in School and Societal Curriculum

School curriculum is a key site for understanding how anti-Black racism was anchored as a construct of white supremacy. We conceptualize school curriculum as any text that conveys academic knowledge in a learning environment—whether in textbooks, children's literature, poems, nursery rhymes, maps, etc. The specific context of schools informs the effectiveness of curricular spaces to reproduce anti-Black racial ideologies. The making and remaking of anti-Black discourses has the capacity to instill in students a set of truths about Black people. Because children enter school as young as 3, how anti-Blackness is framed through received curricula knowledge is particularly dangerous. Schools are spaces where students receive knowledge about academic disciplines, including language, math, history, and geography. This knowledge is often not presented as contested or partial, but rather as the "truth" about particular disciplines (Apple, 2014). Students are expected to acquire this knowledge and then show evidence of its acquisition through the use of standardized tests. Thus, knowledge in school curriculum holds a powerful, hegemonic quality.

For example, Black scholars and activists throughout the twentieth century addressed the long-standing concerns around exposing Black children to stereotypical or myopic depictions of Black people in school curriculum (Au, Brown & Calderon, 2016; Grant, Brown & Brown, 2015). This literature typically noted that children were impressionable and particularly vulnerable to viewing the curriculum they received as truth. When this knowledge positions Blackness in an anti-Black fashion, it anchors in place for students, myopic meanings of Blackness and Black people.

We argue that anti-Blackness in curriculum—both historically and in the contemporary context—explicitly made Black people into what Charles Mills (1998) calls a sub-person. In this context, the white supremacist discourse of the post-Reconstruction Era utilized the space of schools to proffer anti-Black ideas. An example of this is found in textbooks during the early twentieth century that regularly portrayed racial violence as a rational choice for the South to regain control of the South (Brown & Brown, 2015).

Anti-Blackness also persisted in making Black people sub-human through its capacity to include and exclude stories about Black history and life. After Reconstruction and into the early to mid-twentieth century, it was common to see negative images of African American in popular culture, an important form of curriculum that impacted school knowledge. Sterling Brown (1933) found that popular culture helped shape the public imagination about Black people during the early twentieth century. It was in the context of popular culture that authors were given great flexibility to produce fictions about Black life. Similarly, educational texts and school materials, including poetry, songs, and children's literature produced some of the most graphic anti-Black images of the early twentieth century.

This was most prominent in the book *Ten Little Niggers*. This book was intended as a counting game or song to help students understand number sequencing and order. *Ten Little Niggers* told the story of ten Black boys portrayed through a racist white imagination of Black life. On each page, Blacks have exaggerated lips, protruding eyes, watermelon smiles, short twisted hair, and ragged clothes. Black children were the depicted as "pickaninnies." Michelle Martin's (2004) here powerfully articulates the context of the *Ten Little Niggers*:

> This song, written in the United States but popularized in England, became wildly popular in both countries if the proliferation of different versions is any indication. Like "There Were Ten in the Bed" and "Ninety-Nine Bottles of Beer on the Wall," this musical story tells of elimination, but in the case of *Ten Little Niggers*, it is human beings that are successively eliminated—literally. For instance most versions of this tale begin in this way: "Ten Little Nigger Boys went out to dine; One choked his little self, and that left nine." … In most versions of this book prior to the 1940s, seven of the ten characters meet untimely and grizzly deaths. (p. 21)

What *Ten Little Niggers* illustrates is the troubling and powerful ways anti-Blackness was normalized. To place the piccaninny characterization directly in the text and songs for children, helped to naturalize the meaning of Blackness for young children. However, *Ten Niggers* helped to sustain a kind of anti-Blackness beyond simply the explicit debasement of Black life. *Ten Little Niggers* also helped to make implicit the value of Blackness without having to present any intent or purpose for portraying Black people as piccaninnies. In this context Black was linked to minstrels and piccaninnies. The depiction of Blackness became fundamental to the idea of having a counting game as part of the pedagogical space.

During the first half of the twentieth century, this kind of tacit ontological understanding of Blackness and Africa as comprising enslaved peoples, the uncivilized, servants, brutes, or minstrels was also a hallmark of the curricular discourses in textbooks. However, during and after the civil rights movement, meanings of Blackness shifted, where the crimes of racial violence would either completely disappear or they would be placed in school texts in ways that left intact the stable narrative of American exceptionalism (Brown & Brown, 2010).

The presence of anti-Blackness in school curriculum has continued to manifest in contemporary school curriculum. In an examination of how racial violence targeted against African Americans was depicted in the then most recently adopted Texas state social studies textbooks (i.e., 2004), Brown & Brown (2010) found that racism against Black people was positioned as simply "bad men doing bad things." This stands in contrast to understandings of racism as a structural and institutional factor that was predicated on the anti–Black, dehumanizing positioning of Black people in the U.S.

The process of anti–Blackness was accomplished through the construction of ahistorical narratives in school curriculum that disconnected the past from the present. Black people, and the inequalities they faced in society, have no structural/institutional ties to past or present injustices in society. When either erasing the institutional ties to anti-Black racism (e.g., lynching, incarceration, and racial antagonism) or rending it as simply the predilections of a few "bad men doing bad things," (Brown & Brown, 2010) the present societal effects of Black suffering (e.g. poverty, miseducation, etc., as opposed to curricular Black suffering) too often is attributed to the individual choices and actions of African Americans.

This enduring feature of history is important to theorizing anti–Black racism and its concomitant suffering. First, it is dehumanizing to fail to acknowledge the myriad ways that Black people lived in and shaped U.S. life—e.g., farmed land, constructed roads, fought in wars, designed and built the capital city. This places Black people outside of the arc of American value and citizenry and made them into to non–citizens deserving of whatever they receive in the present in terms of racial inequality. Second, failing to mention the existence of racial suffering, or to portray racial violence as solely the act of corrupt social actors, diminishes the gravity of anti–Black racism. Anti–Black racism is positioned as random and only impactful on the victims of such crimes. We argue that histories of anti–Black suffering, whether loss of life or dispossession of Black material growth (e.g. Tulsa Rights), must be understood as having a defining impact on Black people's lives in a contemporary context. However, such constructs have never gone uncontested. In the section that follows, we show how curriculum was a central space to challenge the ideologies of anti–Black racism.

## Spaces of Resistance against Anti-Black Racism

The historical context of resistance in school curriculum played out in the context of Black intellectual thought, primarily through scholarly writing. This work brought to light the irrational forms of racial knowledge portrayed about Black life in K-12 school curriculum. The most prominent example was visible through the curricular project of Carter G. Woodson (Brown, 2010). With the creation of the Association of Negro Life and History in 1915, Woodson sought to engage two pursuits. First, to bring to light how white curriculum writers often served a propagandist role in trying to make Black Americans the descendants of a savage, history-less people or as non-contributors to the American narrative. Second, to produce curricular materials that accurately portrayed the life and history of African Americans.

The writings of authors such as Anna Julia Cooper, W. E. B Du Bois and Charlotte Hawkins Brown (Grants et al., 2015) also offered cogent critiques of the problems with school curriculum and teaching. These writings highlighted the assumptions and representations of Black life represented in school knowledge. Common across the scholarship in the twentieth century is a searing critique of the troubling narratives told about Black life through exclusion and inclusion in school curriculum. These critiques were leveled at the missing, partial and in the later twentieth century, additive, multicultural content tacked on to school curriculum that failed to transform the knowledge that students received.

The above critiques often came through what Jared Sexton (2011) has termed "outer spaces" or those spaces where formal school curricular knowledge was directly challenged. These outer spaces were reflected in Black periodicals, Black universities, Black political organizations and later in more culturally inclusive textbooks. Through these alternative scholarly spaces, scholars illuminated the missing and partial histories of slavery, Jim Crow and anti-Black racism as a whole. This work has highlighted how African Americans contributed to the growth and prosperity of American society (Grant, Brown, & Brown, 2015). In addition to scholarly outer spaces, African Americans have also created and used Black bookstores, cultural and community centers (Ball, 2000), and religious institutions (e.g., churches, mosques) (Watkins, 1993) as alternative, counter-hegemonic spaces to disrupt anti-Black knowledge. Art forms such as music (Akom, 2009) and spoken word poetry (Fisher, 2008) also serve as outer-space genres that allow for creative resistance and transgression against anti-Black curriculum knowledge.

## Final Thoughts

In this chapter we have argued that anti-Black racism reflects a kind of Black suffering that Black students encounter in school curriculum. We recognize the powerful racial apparatus school curriculum offers to sustain anti-Black racism over time. Thus, while collectively we show the changing ways African American are portrayed from one historical period to another, anti-Blackness fundamentally endured through the inclusion and exclusion of African Americans in the American curriculum. Yet in spite of these conditions, African Americans have consistently critiqued and challenged the content and context of school curriculum. They have also consistently fostered alternative, resistant spaces of African American life and histories.

Drawing from a Blackcrit lens, we argue that school curriculum plays a vital role in anchoring the meanings of anti-Black racism. Race and racism have been a constant feature of school curriculum. In one sense, school curriculum helped to bolster existing ideologies of racism. Curriculum making through the blatant removal and silencing of African Americans' histories and contributions in the US American curriculum, then, is both a dangerous and hopeful space for anchoring and naturalizing meanings of Black people and Black life. It is this paradox that punctuates both the terror and hope of Black life in the U.S.

## References

Akom, A. A. (2009). Critical hip hop pedagogy as a form of liberatory praxis. *Equity & Excellence in Education, 42*(1), 52–66.

Apple, M. W. (2014). *Official knowledge: Democratic education in a conservative age.* New York: Routledge.

Au, W., Brown, A. L. & Calderon, L., (2016). *Reclaiming the multicultural roots of the U.S. curriculum: Communities of color and official knowledge in education.* New York: Teachers College Press.

Ball, A. F. (2000). Empowering pedagogies that enhance the learning of multicultural students. *Teachers College Record, 102*(6), 1006–1034.

Bell, D. A. (1976). Racial remediation: An historical perspective on current conditions: *The Notre Dame Lawyer,* 52(1), 5–29.

Brown, A. L. (2010) Counter-memory and race: An examination of African American scholars' challenges to early 20th century K-12 historical discourses. *Journal of Negro Education, 79*(1), 54–65.

Brown, A. L. (2018). From subhuman to human kind: Implicit bias, racial memory, and Black males in schools and society. *Peabody Journal of Education,* 93(1), 52–65. https://doi.org/10.1080/0161956X.2017.1403176

Brown, A. L., & Brown, K. D. (2010). Strange fruit indeed: Interrogating contemporary textbook representations of racial violence towards African Americans. *Teachers College Record, 112* (1), 31–67.

Brown, A. L. & Brown, K. D. (2015). The more things change, the more they stay the same: Excavating race and *enduring racisms* in U.S. Curriculum. *Teachers College Record,* 117 (14), 103–130.

Brown, S. A. (1933). Negro character as seen by white authors. *The Journal of Negro Education, 2*(2), 179–203.

Dumas, M. J., & ross, k. m. (2016). "Be Real Black for Me." Imagining BlackCrit in Education. *Urban Education, 51*(4), 415–442.

Fisher, M. T. (2008). *Black literate lives: Historical and contemporary perspectives.* New York: Routledge.

Grant, C. A., Brown, K. D. & Brown, A. L. (2015). *Black intellectual thought in education: The missing traditions of Anna Julia Cooper, Carter G. Woodson and Alain Locke.* New York: Routledge.

Martin, M. (2004). *Brown gold: Milestones of African American children's books, 1845–2002.* New York: Routledge.

Mills, C. (1997). *The racial contract.* Ithaca, NY: Cornell University Press.

Mills, C. W. (1998). *Blackness visible: Essays on philosophy and race.* Ithaca, NY: Cornell University Press.

Omi, M., & Winant, H. (2014). *Racial formation in the United States.* New York: Routledge.

Sexton, J. (2011). The social life of social death: On Afro-Pessimism and Black Optimism. *InTensions, 5*(1), 1–47.

Watkins, W. (1993). Black curriculum orientations: A preliminary inquiry. *Harvard Educational Review, 63*(3), 321–339.

Wilderson, F. B. (2010). *Red, white & black: Cinema and the structure of U.S. antagonisms.* Durham, NC: Duke University Press.

# 9

# KISSING COUSINS

## Critical Race Theory's Racial Realism and Afropessimism's Social Death

*Kevin Lawrence Henry, Jr. and Shameka N. Powell*

Where might one start in discussing the protracted suffering and gratuitous violence Black people experience in the United States, as an everyday, normalized aspect of our existence? Certainly, we know Black people are more than the diurnal racial antagonisms that saturate our lives, but the fact of the matter is after a cataclysmic race war over chattel slavery in the 1860s and over a century of "racial reforms," the United States continues to structure itself on white dominance and supremacy. As such, the lives of Black people remain imbued by these harsh realities and the effects can be seen on indicators of health, wealth, education, or in disproportionate rates of incarceration. We must meditate on such suffering, as turning our heads neither absolves or eradicates it. We are reminded of Michael Dumas' (2014) words that "[i]t is (enough) to make empirical and theoretical space for attention to loss, to meditate on what it means to experience disregard and lack and betrayal" (pp. 4–5). As we make space for such meditations, the traces of white supremacy become more visible; its legibility makes clear the force of its anti-Black hand. It makes apparent, as Calvin Warren (2017) does in describing Hortense Spillers' notion of *hieroglyphics of the flesh*, "the intoxication of unchecked power and destructive maneuvering over the captive body" (p. 391). Conceptually, then, how does one begin to write of a grammar of violence? This chapter aims to briefly explore two theoretical interventions, Critical Race Theory and Afropessimism, that have given space to not only Black suffering but also the white violence that precedes it.

More specifically, in this chapter we aim to borrow Tate's notion of "paradigmatic kinship," reading "invertedly" to discuss the "paradigmatic kinship" between Bellian CRT and Afropessimism. Specifically, we argue that Bellian *racial realism* and Afropessimism's *social death* constructs share an intellectual connection.

## A Paradigmatic Kinship

In William Tate's (1997) review of critical race theory in education he provides a genealogy of critical race theory and its application in the law. Beyond an expression of the historical and theoretical foundations of the theory, Tate explains the law's connection to education. In what he terms as a "paradigmatic kinship," Tate explores how two seemingly disconnected fields, education and the law, are connected in being sites of social reproduction. Tate (1997) went to describe this paradigmatic kinship as "how both educational research and legal structures contribute to existing belief systems and to legitimating social frameworks and policy that result in educational inequities for people of color" (p. 197). Crucially, for Tate, we are to understand how two central formations are organized around the specter of race. Notions of race map onto bodies, laws, policy, space with resulting stratifications (Wynter, 1995). In other words, how race is epistemologically rendered, paradigmatically placed, or discursively articulated is portrayed in the material realities that Black people experience and, more often than not, suffer. The paradigmatic kinship that cocoons the law and education is premised upon a dehumanization of Black people. The premise is instantiated by "political, scientific, and religious theories relying on racial characterizations and stereotypes" that legitimate the ideological and political order (p. 199). In fewer words, the paradigmatic kinship maintains power relations relying on white dominance and supremacy, as well as anti-Blackness.

In Tate's analysis, he focuses on the "inferiority paradigm" which ultimately situates Black people as structurally less than and inferior in all capacities—biologically, genetically, and otherwise. As such, resulting inequitable accumulations and distributions are normalized; domination in both large scale and everyday acts is not aberrant. It is standard operating procedure. One way this materializes in education and law, according to Tate, is in the characterization of "raced people as intellectually inferior" which raises "doubts about the benefit of equitable social investment in education and other social services" (p. 202). In Tate's approximation, the negative construction of people of color—and for the purposes of this chapter Black people—leads to disinvestment. The link among the ontological, epistemological, and axiological becomes clear. Black people, whose existence is constructed and known as other and abject are devalued. Our devaluation allows for a host of dominations and oppressions to unfurl (Henry, forthcoming). Within such a racial hierarchy, inequity makes sense and white power is sustained and reproduced.

Tate suggests a theory of intervention is needed to explain the role of race in education and the law. CRT is the theory that is proffered. This is where we would like to invert Tate's notion of paradigmatic kinship. Here, as opposed to drawing the connection between two institutional fields—law and education—that are based on white supremacy, we want to connect two theoretical fields—critical race theory and Afropessimism—that explicate white supremacy and anti-Blackness. There exists a bond between these theoretical camps, which have both experienced their share of critique for their refusal to accept incremental, liberal claims for Black freedom (Pyle, 1999). In fact, while CRT does not have pessimism in its name, it has been categorized as "profoundly pessimistic" (Pyle, 1999, p. 796).

## Social Death and Racial Realism

Afropessimism is a conceptual intervention that examines Black existence in the *afterlife of slavery*. Hartman (2008) writes that the afterlife of slavery is marked by "skewed life chances, limited access to health and education, premature death, incarceration, and impoverishment" (p. 6). In the afterlife of slavery, Black students continue to face an ever-mounting education debt, violent interactions with School Resource Officers (SRO), and education policies that continue to sacrifice Black students' educational well-being to the ever-changing whims of whiteness.

Social death, as Afropessimists engage it, emerged from Orlando Patterson's (1982) expansive comparative study of slavery. Patterson, a sociologist, avers that slavery is *social death*. Social death is marked by "the permanent, violent domination of natally alienated and generally dishonored persons" (Patterson, 1982, p. 9). Rather than being based on relations of forced labor, whereby the enslaved are forced to work, slavery is premised on *domination*. This is an important distinction. "Workers," as a category, can have their labor exploited. Social death precludes subjects from being recognized as human. This distinction is integral when one considers that it is through being recognized as "human" that one can be included in society.

Within a historical US context, Blacks were neither human nor citizen. Rather, they were property to be traded and owned. It was through natal alienation that Blacks existed as "branches without roots," (Hurston, 1937, p. 15) whereby, as Spillers (1987) highlights, "kinship loses meaning, since it can be invaded at any given and arbitrary moment by the property relations" (p. 74). In the afterlife of slavery, Black still equals slave in America. In pointing out the specificity of anti-Blackness, Dumas and ross (2016) write "antiblackness is not simply racism against Black people. Rather, antiblackness refers to a broader antagonistic relationship between blackness and the (possibility) of humanity" (p. 429). Paradoxically, Blackness is cast outside of humanity at the same time that it is the foundation for others' humanity. The social death of the Black body is the foundation upon which whiteness and civil society are created and maintained.

Afropessimism and its social death concept foster a paradigmatic shift in the way we are to understand structural domination and violence in a US context and schools. As a conceptual intervention for example, social death explains the recent recordings of Black youth being slammed, dragged, and punched by school officials or institutional agents as par for the course in the afterlife of slavery. Stated differently, violence visited upon the bodies of numerous Black youth not as an aberration but as a perpetual pattern (Henry, 2017).

The perpetual pattern of white violence is what connects the social death concept to a Bellian racial realist perspective. A racial realist perspective moves us away from pollyannaish views of a society structured in dominance to one which sees how deeply entrenched and pervasive racism actually is. Bell's views, often considered pessimistic, highlights the structural position of Black people and the permanence of our position as the "unthought" (Hartman & Wilderson, 2003). Bell (1991) comments,

> Black people will never gain *full* [our emphasis] equality in this country. Even those Herculean efforts we hail as successful will produce no more than temporary 'peaks of progress,' short-lived victories that slide into irrelevance as racial patterns adapt in ways that maintain white dominance. This is a hard-to-accept fact that all history verifies. (pp. 373–374)

At its heart, racial realism is a concept of CRT that aims to explain the macro-position and structural location of Blacks. The processes and mechanisms of racism may alter, but its hierarchical structure remains durable, particularly as it relates to anti-Blackness. That is to say, while individual progress may take place and policies may shift and change, the majority of Black people remain in a "racial time warp" where we are told to believe "that the disadvantages we suffer must be caused by our deficiencies" (Bell, 2004, p. 187). A racial realist perspective ultimately understands that Black suffering, Black death—be it fast or slow—is an accepted and routinized aspect of the state. Moreover, embedded within a racial realist perspective is that full equality is impossible because white accumulative, parasitic structures, which includes the white body, relies on the dispossession and dehumanization of Black bodies and spaces (Henry, 2016; Wynter, 1995). This was most evident in chattel slavery where enslaved Africans are situated as laboring property, as fungible, disposable objects coming from a "Dark Continent." Blackness, through the technology of anti-Blackness, is made to be unmade. Simply, Blacks are the structural prerequisite for the figure of white (hu)man (Wilderson, 2010). Blacks come into being structurally to be effaced discursively and materially for white survival. Therefore, in a Bellian racial realist perspective, the permanence of Black subordination is neither shocking nor unimagined. Full equality would require actual legibility of humanity in a state that thrives on Black vulnerability, objectification, and "property" management.

Because Blackness is understood as the non-human and others' humanity is gained by distancing from Blackness, Afropessimism centers a *Black/non-Black* binary. The centrality of white supremacy and its machinations differ when one juxtaposes racial realism and social death of Afropessimism. Whereas racial realism offers that white supremacy is the organizing schema through which racial domination occurs, viewed through an Afropessimism understanding, anti-Blackness is the organizing principle.

In each of our work we examine how white supremacy and anti-Blackness have manifested within and across education, broadly conceptualized. In exploring mechanisms of structural and institutional racism within American high schools, Powell (2016) illuminates how Black students are made blameworthy for their "systematic exclusion" from viable educational opportunities. Black students are made to bear the brunt of structural and ideological forces that deem them disposable at the same time that their systematic exclusion anchors opportunities of inclusion for other students. In Henry's (2016) work on post-Katrina New Orleans, the mass firing of nearly 7,500 Black teachers exemplifies notions of racial realism and social death. In order to make space for the chartering of New Orleans schools, Black educators were constructed as criminal and lazy and treated as surplus in the ever-expanding desires of racialized neoliberal restructuring. Black educators were rendered intellectually and pedagogically inferior and "sacrificing" them and their union lubricated the arrival of mostly white Teach for America (TFA) staff. While the educators did seek legal recourse, they ultimately lost the lawsuit and received no remedy. The violence of the act is normalized with no legal injury seen in the state's eyes. These Black educators, who were "dead-to-others," realized clearly that in the end, "the law punishes but does not protect, disciplines but does not defend" (Cacho, 2012, p. 8).

## Coda

Both racial realism and social death may prove to be difficult theoretical and conceptual positions for scholars to take up. Bellian racial realist contend that "racial equality is, in fact, not a realistic goal" (Bell, 1992, p. 363). Racial realism and social death take as a central starting point that racism, as a form of domination, is malleable and never-ending. Both concepts index the enduring precarious structural position of Black people, as the dictates of white accumulation in both political and libidinal economies require. The refutation of "rights" and ontological status for Black people endows whites/whiteness. It is what allows Jared Sexton (2008) to state, "if, in the economy of race, whiteness is a form of money-the general equivalent or universal standard of value-then blackness is its gold standard, the bottom-line guarantee represented by hard currency" (p. 30).

Ultimately, we are left with two theoretical interventions that aim to make legible grammars of violence. Because the ideological, material, and psychological forces that oppress and dispossess Black people are ever-changing, nuanced theoretical/conceptual interventions are needed. In this chapter, we have begun to identify links between two conceptual constructs that do that. Future research should consider the connections between Critical Race Theory and

Afropessimism. However, beyond contributing to the paucity of education literature that traces an intellectual kinship between CRT and Afropessimism, this chapter leaves us with the crucial question of "what do we do next in 'a nice filed like education'?" Racial realism and social death as constructs push us toward clarity regarding domination in the United States and provokes us to extinguish policy and pedagogic practices that reinscribe stratification and anti–Blackness. It pushes us to resist anti–Blackness and liberal fantasies. As such, educators and policymakers must grapple with the *specific* deep, everyday, normalized violence Black students, families, and educators face and *continually* work to dismantle it. Racial realism and social death frees us to imagine, hope, and build new futures rooted in Black liberation and freedom knowing that our survival, joy, and love requires us to, as Toni Morrison (1973) notes, "set about creating something else to be" (p. 52).

## References

Bell, D. (1991). Racial realism. *Connecticut Law Review*, 24, 363–380.

Bell, D. (2004). *Silent covenants: Brown v. Board of Education and the unfulfilled hopes for racial reform*. Oxford: Oxford University Press.

Cacho, L. M. (2012). *Social death: Racialized rightlessness and the criminalization of the unprotected*. New York: New York University Press.

Dumas, M. J. (2014). "Losing an arm": Schooling as site of black suffering. *Race Ethnicity and Education*, 17, 1–29.

Dumas, M. J., & ross, k. m. (2016). "Be Real Black for Me": Imagining BlackCrit in education. *Urban Education*, *51*(4), 415–442.

Hartman, S. (2008). *Lose your mother: A journey along the Atlantic slave route*. New York: Farrar, Straus and Giroux.

Hartman, S. & Wilderson III, F. B. (2003). The position of the unthought: An interview with Saidiya Hartman conducted by Frank B. Wilderson, III. *Qui Parle*, *13*(2), 183–201.

Henry, K. L., Jr. (2016). Discursive violence and economic retrenchment: Chartering the sacrifice of Black educators in post-Katrina New Orleans. In J. K. Donnor and T. L. Affolter (Eds.), *The charter school solutions: Distinguishing fact from rhetoric* (pp. 80–98). New York: Routledge.

Henry, K. L., Jr. (2017). A review of Get Out: On White terror and the Black body. *Equity & Excellence in Education, 50*(3), 333–335.

Henry, K. L., Jr. (forthcoming). Zones of nonbeing: Abjection, white accumulation, and neoliberal school reform.

Hurston, Z. N. (1937/2006). *Their eyes were watching God*. New York: Harper Perennial.

Ladson-Billings, G., & Tate IV, W. F. (1995). Toward a critical race theory of Education. *Teachers College Record*, *97*(1), 47–68.

Morrison, T. (1973). *Sula*. New York: Penguin Books.

Patterson, O. (1982). *Slavery and social death*. Cambridge, MA: Harvard University Press.

Powell, S. (2016). Relying on local contexts to foster and thwart Black student academic success: An ethnographic account of teachers fostering academic success for (some) Black students. In *New directions in educational ethnography: Shifts, problems, and reconstruction* (pp. 97–120). Somerville, MA: Emerald Group Publishing.

Pyle, J. J. (1999). Race, equality, and the rule of law: Critical race theory's attack on the promise of liberalism. *Boston College Law Review, 40*(3), 787–827.

Sexton, J. (2008). *Amalgamation schemes: Antiblackness and the critique of multiracialism.* Minneapolis, MN: University of Minneapolis Press.

Spillers, H. J. (1987). Mama's baby, papa's maybe: An American grammar book. *Diacritics, 17*(2), 65–81.

Tate, W. F. (1997). Critical race theory and education: History, theory, and implications. *Review of Research in Education, 22*, 195–247.

Warren, C. (2017). Onticide: Afropessimism, nigger #1, and surplus violence. *GLQ: A Journal of Lesbian and Gay Studies, 23*(3), 391–418.

Wilderson III, F. B. (2010). *Red, white & black: Cinema and the structure of US antagonisms.* Durham, NC: Duke University Press.

Wynter, S. (1995). 1492: A new world view. In V.L. Hyatt and R. Nettleford (Eds.), *Race, discourse, and the origin of the Americas: A new world view* (pp. 5–57). Washington, D.C.: Smithsonian Institution Press.

# PART III
# Research Vignettes

# 10

# SEEKING RESISTANCE AND RUPTURE IN "THE WAKE"

## Locating Ripples of Hope in the Futures of Black Boys

*Roderick L. Carey*

How do teenaged Black boys imagine their future lives beyond high school? Drawing from Afropessimism, I consider this question by focusing on the ways one teenaged Black boy, who lived and learned in an urban context within the United States, imagined making his life beyond his present conditions, while being caught up in what Christina Sharpe (2016) references as "the wake"— or, the everlasting, seemingly immovable afterlife of slavery. By harkening an Afropessimism that reflects the containment, punishment, and captivity imbued by the embodiment of *Blackness*, a symbol for the less-than-human being condemned always to death, I employ Sharpe's conceptualization of wake given its multiple imageries. For Sharpe, wakes describe processes for mourning losses, the sometimes-perilous tracks left by boats, or the bodily disturbances caused by passing vessels. Wake also, and thankfully, means being awake and conscious. Thus, *wake work*, considers not solely Black social death, but the life livable for Black people enmeshed perpetually in uneased-ness, mourning, and demise (Sharpe, 2016).

In this chapter, I probe the experiences of Samuel (pseudonym), a 17-year-old Black boy who I studied during his junior year at a college-preparatory high school in an urban U.S. context. As Samuel imagined his future, he did so while weighing personal ambition with familial responsibility. Through an Afropessimistic lens, Samuel's hope for a future, free of the social mechanisms that kept him and his family bound to poverty and despair, reflected a radical imagining amidst a seemingly impossible milieu. With Afropessimism's appeal to the impossibility and destruction of Blackness historically, presently, and even in futurities, this chapter grapples with the following: how do Black boys, like Samuel, simultaneously live in the wake and resist it, and through resistance, rupture its unrelenting force by imagining and making futures for themselves on their own terms? And, how can educators through co-envisioning, support the future-oriented imagining of Black boys and young men?

## Samuel's Life in the Wake

Samuel and I met in 2013 when I studied the hopes and aspirations of nine Black and Latino adolescent boys and young men at his school, Metro Collegiate Public Charter School (Metro). Metro was a highly lauded, beautifully renovated, college-preparatory school in a U.S., Mid-Atlantic city. Standing in stark contrast to other city schools that offered uglier classrooms, seemingly burned-out teachers, and chancier likely hoods of securing college-enrollment for its students, Metro attracted racially and ethnically diverse working-class families seeking a better future via college admittance for their children.

Similar to the other Black and Latino high school junior and senior boys and young men that I studied that year, Samuel's 17-year-old life was fraught with neighborhood violence and poverty. Though brilliant and kind, his quiet and unassuming nature made him a target for street attacks. Neighborhood teens sometimes "jumped" and robbed Samuel, although he rarely had anything worth stealing, due in part to his family's financial restraints. When I first interviewed Samuel, his glasses were frosted with scratches and snapped along the frame. However, with tape and some metal-bending, ingenious and resourceful Samuel made them work, as his unemployed mother could not afford a new pair. His often-disconnected cell phone left him out of the social loop his peers maintained on Twitter and Instagram. Lanky and sometimes aloof, academically decent, and unobtrusive Samuel preferred video-gaming and skateboarding to the organized athletics favored by other Black boy peers.

## Imagining through the Wake

Over the course of four interviews, Samuel envisioned that after high school, his ideal life would begin with attending a safe, serene college campus far away from his urban community. In describing what college symbolized, Samuel noted, "... people and things make me want to leave, and college is that leap out of the city area, or out of the *ghetto* for me. College is where I start my life over again, actually ..." His present existence in his urban community was mired by violence, and his home life with his two other brothers, was noisy and congested, allowing minimal peace to think, to be himself. The future life he yearned for reflected a radical hope, an aspirational vision, or what Sharpe (2016) refers to as "Black optics" or "the insistent Black visualsonic resistance" (p. 21) to the non-being and subsequent non-imagining demanded of life in the wake. The life Samuel imagined reflected at best a life outside of the wake, but more realistically and precisely a significant rupture or resistance of Black being in the wake. This unlikelihood to escape the wake echoes with the impossibility for Black people to ever leave the containment of Black suffering, symbolically and materially embodied in Samuel's ghetto.

Even if he departed home for college, Samuel doubted his agency to enact his life vision on his own terms. Looming always was the responsibility he felt to save family members still in his ghetto or *hood* (as I will reference to avoid the deficit implications of the term *ghetto*), which was evidenced when Samuel said, "So I kind of think that growing older, I might have to watch over my twin brother, because he has to deal with some things that might get him kicked out of the house and just other things ... I think I might have to put my life on hold for him" (Carey, 2018, p. 18). Though his family supported his college-going (Carey, 2016, 2018), family-based push/pull, go/stay factors undergirded Samuel's anticipated straddling of two worlds; a serene college world and the perpetual and inescapable hood. Here, Samuel not only lived in the wake, but also held a wake, or mourned being limited and confined within it (Sharpe, 2016). Samuel expected having his life interrupted to redirect energy and resources away from his college ambitions onto his struggling brother and subsequently mourned the loss of his envisioned peace, free from familial struggle, free from saving people, free from his hood. Thus, Samuel's college freedom will be ungraspable, as he perpetually straddles life there, with the life he left in the city, hallmarked by the continual suffering of family like his brother. While college was an imagined, scenic context for him to create life on his terms, a freeing, safe place where he could start anew and find peace, Samuel could not imagine achieving these visions for himself while family members suffered back home.

After college, Samuel hoped to secure an engineering job and desired a simple, peace-filled life. In Samuel's words, his dream was to "have my own house, like just be isolated." The cluster and clamor accompanying his life in urban poverty exhausted him, and he longed for a career he liked and his own space to be isolated from all that brought him strife as a young boy and teenager. In imagining his future hopes further, Samuel described his desires for, "... just not having to worry about things that I shouldn't have to worry about." In finding his way out, mentally and physically, Samuel always returned to descriptions of peace, stresslessness, and control. There was an abiding freedom at the root of his hopes, a freedom that was mostly tied to simply worrying about himself only.

In spite of so many devastating social realities rooted in the perpetual demise of Black people, Samuel imagined his future elaborately, worked to make his life on his terms, and by doing so reflected a radical, almost unimaginable hope for his life. As Samuel envisioned the future, he remained trapped, bound by, and bound to the same devastation that he sought to envision his way out of. This *hope beyond*, in some ways was almost in-articulable, because that *beyond* implied a fettering to that which he wanted to escape—here, read as his family's struggles in the hood. Samuel's imaginings for his own life were bound up in the perpetual pain and suffering of those who he will leave behind. Living itself, especially the type of living that resists present-day pleasures for the hope of future securities is an act of a radical hope imbued in Black boys and young men like Samuel, let alone planning and enacting. Simply imagining a future that is so divergent from anything in close proximity to Black boys in urban settings is a radical act. Boys and young men of color that imagine like this refuse acquiescence to the societal need for their perpetual failure, for their inevitable demise.

As an adolescent Black boy, Samuel's future life concept was tied to his own skillfulness to creatively imagine, if not necessarily enact, his most perfect future outcome. Samuel's imaginary also reflects his realization of the seeming impossibility of his future life goals for peace and isolation, because poverty, violence, and other anti-Black elements will remain, even if they shift in their placement in his life. Thus, as he imagines for his own future life, even if he achieves a measure of agentic peace for himself, he will never be removed from the poverty and other effects of anti-Black solidarity that contributes to the suffering of those within his low-income family. However, his insistence on actually imagining, and using the tool of education to make his life, reflects Black being and finding resistance "in the wake" (Sharpe, 2016).

## Afropessimism in the School Lives of Black Boys: Implications and Conclusions

For Afropessimism, Black individuals are sentient beings, although the entire world around them operates with an anti-Black solidarity (Wilderson, 2010). Similarly, with so much school and societal co-constructed failure at the ready for Black boys at almost every turn their lives take, it appears that educational ventures serving Black boys and young men of color are threaded together with an anti-Black universal commitment. Afropessimism beckons then for an alternative, even transcendental subjectivity (Moten, 2013) for Black boys where he is not demeaned as the cast-off, the proof of Whiteness, and subsequently White superiority. Rather, Black boys and young men may be conceived as original, feeling beings, disassociated from the structures and individuals nearby that not only demand their demise (e.g. Black social death) but also require it for their righteousness, their survival (e.g. fueling Whiteness). The project of Afropessimism then is to explore the possible existences of alternative worlds and futures, given the scope of a perennial demise of Black bodies. This necessary work is that of the educators of Black schoolchildren, whose responsibility, though often unmentioned, is to create future-oriented learning experiences for children whose futures are not only unpromised but also are, and more deviously, unimagined.

In the beginning of this chapter, I considered how one teenaged Black boy hoped and conceptualized his future. Perhaps then, the questions for educators are the following: what mechanisms of societal failure travel through the bloodstreams of Black boys and use their bodies as tools to justify their perpetual demise? And thus, why is it so difficult for educators to imagine the futures of Black boys and young men, free of demise, destruction, and death? Black boys' futures are imagined as threatening and destructive to maintaining a social order of things. Educators stew in these images, which limit imaginations for the unthought-of worlds (see Hartman & Wilderson, 2003) that Black boys can occupy.

Educators—those who consider themselves, radical—must do the work to not only deconstruct their assumptions, and stereotypes of their Black boys, but they must make the necessary move to work in concert with the boys to imagine and build new understandings in relation to them. Given the amount of social imagining and labor demanded of Black boys, educators must share the cognitive load, or *chip-in* on the imagining project with the boys themselves to co-construct a visionary future, unfettered from demise. To begin, educators must turn away from mere survival supports, to those that point to Black boy thriving. Admittedly, the perpetual wake catalyzes a cry for whether or not there is "thriving" while Black. This compels the following questions: Is the educational goal to only help Black boys "survive" in a world that insists on their demise? Is there even an option for thriving, and if so, what questions about moving from Black boy survival to Black boy thriving can drive policy, curriculum, and classroom discourses?

It is essential that schools resist negative tropes and work instead in expansive, humanizing notions of Black boys and young men (Dumas & Nelson, 2016) by stimulating the ingenuity of boys to imagine and then practice creative ways to then enact their aspirations. A next move in asset-based pedagogies is not only the rooting of curriculums responsively in the realities of the boys' lived experiences but also in the worlds they imagine for themselves, drawn, glued-together, colored with crayons, sketched or painted, perhaps. Mindful of all the toxicity shrouding the histories and present-day lives of Black boys and young men, educators must creatively help their students delve deeply into their imagined worlds, sit creatively within future-oriented life projects and always emerge with something whole, novel, something genuinely and comprehensively them.

How can we think differently in relation to the demise and destruction nestled and reproduced within the academic and social failure created for Black boys? How can we create futurities, perhaps in some fictive elsewhere, free of pain and required devastation? And if we arrive, will things be even better over "there?" Can opportunity reside "in the wake?" And, will Black boys and young men ever "live the lives meant to be unlivable" (Sharpe, 2016, p. 22)? Afropessimism calls forth an educational imagination where optimally educators will work alongside Black boys, like Samuel, guiding them as they awaken a future that builds within, imagines throughout, and subsequently, resists the wake.

## References

Carey, R. L. (2016). "Keep that in mind … You're gonna go to college": Family influence on the college going processes of Black and Latino high school boys. *The Urban Review, 48*(5), 718–742. doi:10.1007/s11256-016-0375-8.

Carey, R. L. (2018). "What am I gonna be losing?": School culture and the family based college going dilemmas of Black and Latino adolescent boys. *Education and Urban Society, 50*(3), 246–273. doi:10.1177/0013124517713112.

Dumas, M. J., & Nelson, J. D. (2016). (Re)Imagining Black boyhood: Toward a critical framework for educational research. *Harvard Educational Review, 86*(1), 27–47. doi:10.17763/0017–8055.86.1.27.

Hartman, S. V., & Wilderson, F. B. (2003). The position of the unthought. *Qui Parle, 13*(2), 183–201.

Moten, F. (2013). Blackness and nothingness (mysticism in the flesh). *South Atlantic Quarterly, 112*(4), 737–780. doi:10.1215/00382876–2345261.

Sharpe, C. (2016). *In the wake: On blackness and being.* Durham, NC: Duke University Press.

Wilderson, F. B. (2010). *Red, white, and black: Cinema and the structure of U.S. antagonisms.* Durham, NC: Duke University Press.

# 11

# KNOWLEDGE AND POWER

## A Case Study on Anti-Blackness within Schooling

*Tiffani Marie*

## Shaun

In one of my most memorable sessions with Shaun, he passionately expressed his dreams of traveling the world and studying in Italy to become a "world renowned chef." This day, he was excited that in a week, as part of his culinary program, he would prepare a meal for the former Mayor of San Francisco, Willie Brown. Laugh lines creased through Shaun's deep chocolate skin as he explained his process of preparing to cook for the mayor. As he played with his soft afro, he said, "... I mixed garlic, tomatoes and then I put some black truffle olive oil, black pepper and salt and mixed that up and put it on some bread ... and I called it salsa bruchetta. I would show you some pictures of it on my ipad, but they [school administrators] got it." His pride sat in his shoulders. At 5′11, in the 8th grade, Shaun stood tall, as he assured me that he "had skills." Appreciative of his passion and commitment to the art of cooking, I anticipated the details of his event with Willie Brown in our next meeting.

When I went to visit Shaun for our next weekly meeting, his Science teacher smirked and shared, "he's in the 5th grade." In working to complete my field study, I met with Shaun weekly to document his schooling experiences. This week, instead of articulating the phases of Mitosis, Shaun would return to math chants, silent bathroom signals, and story time. My field notes from that day explained that since Shaun refused to follow his teacher's directions on a recent field trip, he would be placed in a 5th grade classroom, until he was "ready to act like an 8th grader at POWER." When I entered the brightly decorated 5th grade classroom, tiny students participated in their daily routines. Some had the task of paper monitor, in which they swiftly made their rounds and collected student papers. One young student rocked back and forth; her pigtails, with one missing hair tie, swung parallel to her movement. With pressed, crossed legs, she raised her crossed fingers, signaling to her teacher that she needed to visit the restroom. In a corner, sat Shaun, 5'11, stuffed into a small desk, like a monument wedged between plastic and wood. With his head cradled in the crook of his folded arms, ignoring the papers in front of him, thin blue sheets meant to monitor his behavior, Shaun appeared to be cracking beneath the weight of a bent will, threatening to break. There is legacy in the hunch of his back, a history in the curve of his spine, one that has systemically shattered the hope of black boys, leaving them pinned under debris misnamed delinquency, spelled in their names. Shaun's posture embodied a hidden curriculum, and the 5th graders learned through Shaun, what happens when you attempt to straighten your back.

When I was finally able to talk to Shaun in the 5th grade classroom, he shared that he was reprimanded because he chose to speak with his peers, instead of reading silently on a 10-minute train ride. My field notes from the day reflect our conversation:

> Shaun and I had an opportunity to talk and he expressed to me that he felt targeted. He shared that the day before, the 8th grade team were on a field trip to visit College Track, a college preparatory program for high school students. College Track is located on the same street as POWER and traveling to the site required for students to catch the R Train for approximately 10 minutes to make it to the front of College Track. As students were on the train, they were instructed to remain silent and read a book. Shaun said that he did not want to read; so, he sat silently. He was instructed to read by one of his teachers, but refused. He noted that minutes later, many of his peers began to close their books as well and talk to each other; so, he too began to converse with one of his peers. Again, he was addressed for his behavior and mentioned to his teacher that many others were talking. When they arrived at College Track, Shaun and another black boy were separated from their peers and addressed by one of their teachers, Ms. Jargon (a teacher that he noted in our interview that he hated and felt hated him). She instructed the black boys to stop talking and they resisted and continued to critique her decision to separate them from their peers. Ms. Jargon called the acting principal to come get the boys.
>
> Ms. Randy, the acting principal, arrived to pick up Shaun and his friend and as they asked her why they were being brought back to school, according to Shaun, she responded, "don't talk in my car." Shaun expressed that at this point he was ready to go home. Once he arrived at POWER, he was handed over to the transitioning principal and told her that he wanted to go home. She expressed that he had two choices: he could stay at school or he could go home. She shared that if he chose to

go home, he should choose a different school to attend the following day. Shaun called his mother and asked to be transferred to another school and he said that his mother "cursed him out." Shaun was conflicted. If he left school, which he wanted to, according to the school's administrator, he wouldn't be allowed to return; however, Shaun's mother also shared that she wasn't going to transfer him to another school. Shaun left school that day, yet returned the next day. The transitioning principal then told Shaun that if he was serious about his education, he needed to prove it to her. She placed Shaun in a 5th grade classroom with a blue sheet of paper, for 5th grade teachers to monitor his maturation process.

Public shaming is as much a part of the school culture at POWER middle school as bells and uniforms. POWER, a small middle school that serves approximately 250 students, is located in a predominately poor, black region of San Francisco: 73% of their students are African American, 15% Latinx, 9% Pacific Islander and 2% identify as other. Eighty-one percent of POWER students qualify for free or reduced lunch. Over 90% of POWER's teaching staff is white and are recruited from a larger sister program in which they receive only five weeks of training before they work within many of the nation's most underserved schools. In many ways, POWER's demographics reflect the very structure of a colonial regime; the same people are responsible for knowledge production and dissemination. Dark bodies are still subjected to violence as a consequence of their skin and the regulation of such violence is still enforced through the rhetoric of progress. With the presence of colorblind policies, these racisms are more difficult to identify. Within this culture, "new formulations seek to make the social appear natural and ruthless, inequality appear as common sense" (Mullings, 2005, p. 679).

The policing structures that inform POWER middle school's policies also inform Shaun's consciousness as it relates to what he understands as acceptable communal realities. Shaun and I both reside in the Bayview community of San Francisco. So, when we purchase soap from the local convenient store, which is located down the street from Shaun's residential complex, we must ask permission from store employees to unlock the shelves containing soap. The procedure goes as follows: patrons must decide which locked items they need well before entering the store, as any misstep of this process could subject one to more violence. Then, patrons must contact a store clerk to unlock the requested items. These items include pregnancy tests, sanitary napkins, soap, razors, and even baby formula. Once the requested items are unlocked, they must be handed to the store clerk who then walks the items to the counter. Items may only be touched upon payment. In the candy aisle, patrons must lift a cover to obtain their candy. When the lift is raised, an electronic voice blares from implanted speakers, instructing patrons to close the lift. If the lift remains open for more than 10 seconds, an alarm sounds. Shaun is not alarmed throughout this process, particularly because his experiences within his school norm the timing of when and how he can use his body. Essentially, the policies at POWER help normalize the ongoing surveillance of Shaun's every move.

Aside from the constant store surveillance Shaun steps outside into a community that also mirrors a colonial regime. He states,

> You have 13-to-16-year-old boys dropping out of school to sell weed. Some of them are my friends. I'm not gonna lie. I just don't hang out with them that much. When you see this, it limits your possibilities. If they didn't do it, how can I do it? It limits your dreams and goals and everything.

Shaun's community houses the city's vices, a ghetto as a colony if you will. As Tabb (1970) mentions, communities like Shaun's, or black ghettos, are characterized by extremely low employment, police harassment, and exploitation. He states that the "black ghetto stands as a unit apart, an internal colony exploited in a systemic fashion" (Tabb, 1970, p. 21). These spaces are formed through the confinement of black bodies and labor that is exported from their communities to sustain whiteness. The cost of living is much higher in the black ghetto. Shaun's community pays what researchers call a poverty tax, where resources like gasoline, groceries, and even parking meters are priced significantly higher than in nearby white communities. The public sector also mirrors the colonial structure, in that the jobs solely responsible for the safety of the body and intellectual faculty, jobs like police officers and teachers, are largely sustained by white outsiders.

Tabb's analysis provides important commentary surrounding the ways in which communities, or state sanctioned cages, have been constructed in a way that align with Shaun's analysis of his community; they limit residents from adequate resources, affirm their nothingness and keep them bowed to state policies and regulations. Such realities manufacture the *need* for sites like POWER. POWER becomes the best amongst the worst options for poor black people. Teachers at POWER are then paid [well] to manage poor youth. POWER relies on the desolation of the black body to employ and sustain white ownership of knowledge and capital. This framework does not create the conditions for teacher sustainability as it relies upon high teacher turnover in order to secure jobs for newly awaiting [white] preservice teachers. An investment in ending suffering—in teacher sustainability—would mean an investment in putting itself out of business. And that's just not good business. Schools like POWER rely upon failure for job security for their teachers, who after their time within the field (usually under three years), go on to secure advanced jobs in social work, medicine, and the juvenile justice system. Their time served within the hood is an impressive look for pursuing more desired positions. We do not speak of these realities. Rather than acknowledge the complex interrelatedness of black suffering and white sustainability, the language of power often places the onus of change on the oppressed themselves. This approach overestimates the power of the individual, while underestimating the structures that rely upon the lived histories of anti-blackness and white supremacy, for its maintenance.

POWER's schooling processes reflect a larger neoliberal culture that reproduce the community's disenfranchisement; it engages the language of "hard work," "grit" and "delayed gratification" in order to explain away legacies of discriminatory and excluding legislation, gang-injunctions, poverty taxes, and other forms of state sanctioned violence. Indeed, POWER works to norm the conditions by which Shaun operates within the world. The culture of will-breaking that exists within the school often goes unnoticed and understudied. It is a violence that eventually convinces us that our love of learning or even commitment to progress must operate in close proximity to subjugation. There is a certain posture that POWER manufactures in students; it is not one that asserts their uprightness in society, rather one that forces them to bow, to accept the violence that is imposed upon them. Shaun's experiences reflect a unique form of schooling violence that result from the intersections of his race and class. There are certain forms of surveillance and bodily harm that are easier to inflict upon poor black youth. Shaun's experiences are very much about humiliation. POWER's approaches to discipline and punishment are often avoidable by middle class families. These practices rely upon parent fatigue often as a result of extensive work hours, internalized oppression, and even a market of limited communal resources in order to function. Because of his poverty and blackness, Shaun and his family often have to *take what they can get*.

Despite his reality, Shaun desires more. Directly down the street from his school, he participates in a culinary program. In fact, when he is suspended from POWER middle school he develops his craft by attending his cooking courses. Shaun participates on Saturdays often arriving as early as 7:00am and leading peers, some older than him, in learning the art of cooking. Shaun honors the program "because he gets to mix and create things." In Shaun's culinary program, his intellectual faculties are cultivated. He is encouraged to make meaning through experimentation and testing boundaries. His award-winning salsa bruschetta was a product of such innovation. Shaun straightens his back when he explains how proud he was that "everyone was eating from [him]." He identifies his cooking as a way to "give back to his community."

Many of Shaun's teachers are unaware of his participation in his culinary program, despite their commitment to "to develop critical thinking skills and character traits needed for their students to attend the nation's top high schools and colleges." POWER uses social reform as a means to condition poor, black, youth to conform to a capitalist society, rather than preparing students to disrupt it. To be clear, access to higher education serves as an important tool for social transformation. However, such a trajectory, absent critical engagement of the context of urban life, merely works to bank Western values, common core standards and whiteness into poor black students. The complex social conditions surrounding Shaun and other youth require of practitioners a framework that confronts the interconnectedness of Shaun's broken will and the maintenance of a capitalist structure and whiteness. Much like his ancestors, Shaun's body holds a price. It is most valuable broken. It benefits the structure for Shaun to not only bow, but to believe that his bowing is his rightly position within society.

A year later, I interviewed Shaun and asked him to reflect on the time that he was placed into a 5th grade classroom for refusing to read upon command. Shaun states,

> O, that decision was … I was being hard-headed and I loved to always be right … but now I … matured a little bit. I wouldn't say all the way. I'm still growing, still learning … for uh summer school I ended up knowing everything, and all the students didn't know anything … so I believe POWER prepared me the best they could and if I actually paid attention, I could have had a better knowledge of it.

Shaun appeared to be a rendering of white America, lowly and embracing of his wretched orientation.

### References

Mullings, L. (2005). Interrograting racism: Toward an antiracist anthropology. *Annual Review of Anthopology, 34*, 667–693.

Tabb, W. K. (1970). *The Political Economy of the Black Ghetto*. New York: W. W. Norton.

# 12

# DEBATING WHILE BLACK

## Wake Work in Black Youth Politics

*Shanara R. Reid-Brinkley*

In the spring of 2017, Rutgers University's Nick Nave and Devane Murphy, a team of two Black students won the two national policy debate championships (CEDA Nationals and the National Debate Tournament), uniting the crowns for only the second time in policy debate's history. The historic win is the second time, in just four years, that a Black team has achieved a feat that no other team has in the White-dominated activity of competitive policy debate. Policy debate is a tournament style co-curricular activity, where students role-play as agents of the government requiring them to engage in the cost-benefit analysis frame of political decision-making. Black debaters, like the Rutgers' students, are engaged in a direct action protest to contest State role-playing and cost-benefit analysis as inherently anti-Black. Rutgers' achievement is a result of the acceleration of Black presence, Black thought, and Black radical confrontation in competitive college debate, a marriage of theories of anti-blackness and revolutionary activism. This chapter argues that Afropessimism has radical liberatory potential as a heuristic for engaging in political and social activism for Black youths and young adults. Afropessimism's utility in framing anti-blackness as the context from which students emerge into the world need not destroy the beauty of youthful hope, it can instead galvanize a different kind of hope that is generative and sustaining toward dreaming of new futures. In conversation with Christina Sharpe's concept of "wake work" I suggest that Black debaters are developing rhetorical and argumentative strategies to engage anti-blackness and build new relationships to futurity. Using the final round of the 2017 National Debate Tournament as a case study, I demonstrate an example of the timely and productive relationship between Afropessimism and youth activism. In the following section, I discuss Christina Sharpe's theory of "wake work" as a heuristic for engaging in Black political action.

> You talk about violence—but when you walk by us in the hallway you literally have nothing to fucking say to us, but you say that we are part of the fucking community.
>
> *(Murphy, 2017)*

## Afropessimism, Wake Work and Black Political Strategy

Black debaters radically engage the debate community's exclusion of Black students from successful participation, of Black scholarship and of Black political concerns from competition. The strategies of Black Debate practice focus on the political and educational spaces, like competitive debate, that are constituted by Black death. It is an example of, to use Christina Sharpe's terminology, "bringing out the dead," or "wake work" (Sharpe, 2016). Utilizing Saidiya Hartman's discussion of the "afterlife of slavery" (Hartman, 2008, p. 6), Sharpe offers the metaphor of the "wake" as an analytic for thinking about Black life in relation to the structuring relationship of the Black as property. As Sharpe argues, slavery continues and "the holds multiply" (2016, p. 504). Sharpe uses three senses of "in the wake": 1) the disturbance of water during the passage of a ship, 2) a remembrance and honoring of the dead, 3) a bringing to consciousness (2016, pp. 145–146). Using this interpretation of "in the wake" Sharpe explains that wake work is "… interested in plotting, mapping, and collecting the archives of the everyday of Black immanent and imminent death, and in tracking the ways we resist, rupture, and disrupt that immanence and imminence aesthetically and materially" (2016, p. 102). The students are engaged in political wake work seeking to re-conceptualize Black politics against the backdrop of anti-blackness. For Black debaters, there is no form of reparative justice that accounts for anti-blackness as structural antagonism. In this manner, Black Debate as a practice can be characterized by Calvin Warren's notion of "political apostasy," a method of "renouncing" anti-blackness while rejecting the notion that such can resolve the structural antagonism (2015, p. 233). The Black nihilist perspective Warren offers requires a radical spiritual hope unencumbered by political hope. The onset of Black Debate practice theorizes from within the hold, producing a "form of consciousness" toward the political that offers new paths of strategic engagement without any commitment to maintaining civil society (Sharpe, 2016, p. 104). Such an orientation frees Black students to imagine radical practices of confrontation and dreams of Black futurity. What lies "in the wake" of competitive policy debate? How are Black debaters *doing* wake work? In the following section I take two examples from the National Debate Tournament

Final Round to demonstrate wake work in competitive debate. Next, I analyze the central argument in the final round characterizing the current clash of civilizations in debate and the ramifications of building community in debate.

## Framework/Black Framework

The final round of the 2017 National Debate Tournament was not just a competition, it was a referendum on the notion of a universal community and the structural exclusions and fairness issues that characterize the traditions and norms of competitive practice. Georgetown is affirmative in the debate and offer a federal policy toward Alaska as an example of a specific proposal to combat catastrophic climate change. Based on the norms of competition, Georgetown presents a coherent affirmative argument providing an effective stasis point for fair deliberation of the climate change resolution. After the affirmative's speech Rutgers is allowed to cross-examine the speaker. Devane Murphy asks, "When is the first life saved as a result of the aff[irmative]?" (2017). While Georgetown admits that a debate round cannot save lives directly, they argue that discussing climate change policy is a valuable academic conversation. Rutgers then asks a series of questions about Georgetown's relationship as individuals to the people and places targeted by the federal policy they suggest: "Do you know any people in the arctic? Do you know any communities in the arctic? Can you name a family in the arctic?" (Murphy, 2017). While Georgetown answers no to these questions, they argue that a focus on debaters as individuals rather than the policy option they have presented is a distraction from the stasis point they have set for the debate.

Using Afropessimism as a heuristic for engaging the resolution, debaters like Rutgers, reject any affirmation of the United States Federal Government. For these students, the federal government is always an unethical actor. In as much as the resolutional statement requires the affirmative to posit federal government action as an ethical response to public need, the vast majority of Black debaters refuse to take such a position. To combat this refusal to follow competitive norms, the Framework argument developed to confront the disruption of the normative form and content of policy debate competition. Framework debaters (mostly White and non-Black POCs) argue that if a team violates the norms of common practice they reject the normative stasis points for deliberation destroying the educational benefits of policy debate.

Framework has operated as a strategic tool of capture and exclusion of Black thought in competitive debate. However, as "the holds multiply" so too does Black innovation. Rutgers' strategy in the final round took the form of the traditional Framework argument, but using Black thought to revise the content and turn it against the norms of traditional debate. *Black* Framework, Rutgers' strategy, argued that the affirmative must embody their politics and demonstrate how they directly engage in efforts to reduce climate change. Rutgers' argues that Georgetown is disconnected from their politics which is why they can advocate a policy that may affect the people of the Arctic while having little knowledge of those people or their lives. This kind of orientation toward policy action is dangerous, encouraging what Rutgers refers to as "ascetic tourism" by which debaters role-playing policy advocates "tour [the] trauma of various populations without ever acting to alleviate the harm" (Murphy, 2017).

When Georgetown seeks further clarification of *Black* Framework, Rutgers' responds: "We provided an interpretation of what we think debate should look like, the same way in which when you're negative and you read my affirmative and you say we should not be able to do what we do. Very simple" (Murphy, 2017). Georgetown often runs the traditional Framework argument against Black Debate teams who fall outside their interpretation of a fair stasis point for debate about the resolution. Rutgers' turns the tables on Georgetown arguing that the traditional form of policy debate produces poor policy advocates and that Black Debate practice which centers embodied political practice is a superior method of training political advocates. *Black* Framework is an example of political theorizing from the hold. It operates from the perspective that anti-blackness is the stage upon which all political deliberation is played and then strategically identifies a tactic and an exigency for disruption. Rutgers capitalizes on the growing middle majority of judges who agree that Black Debate practice is an effective training tool for political advocacy. The use of *Black* Framework flips the script; it is a jarring (*re*)performance of the acts of exclusion that Black debaters have faced for decades. It took the form of Framework, paired with Black content, to argue that the neo-liberal norms of civil society would no longer get a free pass as the base frame for political negotiation. Rutgers turned a mirror on debate and offered a reflection of itself haunted by the specter of Black death. Arguing *Black* Framework was an act of bringing out the dead.

## Who Gets to Define Community?

> You don't want community, you don't want us here, you have never wanted niggaz here. But guess what, we are here and we are going to unite the motherfucking crowns, we're going to take all your shit and we are going to laugh at you while we fucking do it.
>
> *(Nave, 2017)*

Communal acceptance in policy debate depends on the willingness of the 'other' to *share* the values, practices, and traditions of the community. Black Framework is the technical argument that Rutgers uses to win the debate, but the debate is really about the "aesthetic" and "material" forms of anti-blackness that constitute community relations (Sharpe, 2016). Rutgers spent the first seven minutes of their initial speech "roasting" the opposing team, the White judges, and the White debate community members in the audience. The Rutgers debaters consulted with other members of the Black community before the debate and came up with a list of jokes to tell during the speech. While Rutgers delivers one-line zingers targeted at the White people in the audience, they also pass the microphone to members of the Black community in the audience so that they can participate in the roast. They offer the opposing team the opportunity to participate, but they refuse the offer.

Georgetown counters that the tactic of the first speech is divisive and potentially violent for those who are made uncomfortable being the target of such jokes. During an exchange one of the Georgetown debaters admits they are uncomfortable. Rutgers responds that they are glad Georgetown is uncomfortable and that White discomfort is a good thing. They argue further that there is no "litmus test" for discomfort given that Black people are persistently made to feel uncomfortable in the debate community (Nave, 2017). Rutgers argues that Georgetown's framing of them as violent is "a tactic of whiteness" by which Georgetown "criminalize[s] the flesh of black bodies by identifying that we are the violent ones, but then they get to be the ones that exact violence on the surface of the debate space" (Murphy, 2017). The violence that Rutgers alludes to are the repetitive micro-aggressions and competitive tactics of exclusion. As Rutgers notes, "the community is divided" (Murphy, 2017), and the traditionalists must take responsibility for "your ability to produce violence" (Nave, 2017). Nick Nave goes on to argue that White people feel "so fucking authoritative up in here … Because you get to do what you fucking want, say what you fucking want … Now it's time for Niggaz to do what we want" (2017).

Georgetown fails to grapple with the possibility that not everyone feels a part of the community and that Black people, in particular, are made to feel like they are a threat that must be contained. Traditionalists are unable to understand that when they use Framework to exclude Black argumentation it translates as "Niggers Go Home." Racial micro-aggressions like a refusal to socially engage Black students and coaches or persistent reminders that Black lives do not matter destroys any attempt at community building.

Before the tournament began, a young Black debater from the University of Louisville, Savannah Walker, was tragically killed. The Louisville team was informed of her death during the first national tournament that directly precedes the National Debate Tournament. The Black Debate community was shocked, grieving along with her coaches and team members. During the opening ceremony of the National Debate Tournament, just days later, Savannah was left out of the commemoration of the loss of former or current members. Over the next few days there was an uproar amongst the Black community. After being informed of the "oversight" tournament officials allowed a member of the Black community to honor Savannah during the awards ceremony. During the finals Rutgers' highlights Savannah's absence in the original ceremony, Nick Nave argues:

> "This space is parasitic to Black people, especially Black women. In a world where you don't even fucking remember us at your … awards ceremony, yet you want to … claim community. You can't fucking say our name … You will say Savannah's … name at the end of this shit!"
>
> *(Nave, 2017)*

The Black community in the audience claps furiously during this part of the speech, together with Rutgers, they mourn Savannah's loss and refuse to allow the community to make her death invisible; a bringing out the dead.

## Conclusion

What is happening on the college debate circuit is replicating itself at the high school level as Black Debate practice has spread like wildfire amongst Black and Brown youth. More than fifteen years after this movement began in policy debate, its alumni have gone on to run their own non-profits and political action committees, they are young academics and teachers, they are community activists and entrepreneurs. As it has grown it has fostered the development of a community grounded in networks of support and intellectual and artistic creativity. The traditional, majority-white and cis-heteronormative debate community may act to exclude Black presence, if not Black people, but in doing so it has ushered in a critical mass of Black thinkers, teachers and students. Black Debate is a bringing out of the politically, socially and literally dead; it is wake work in the afterlife of slavery; it is a battle cry of the young to STAY WOKE. It is important as academics and educators that we listen and pay attention.

## Bibliography

Hartman, S. (2008). *Lose Your Mother: A Journey along the Atlantic Slave Route*. New York: Farrar, Strauss and Giroux.

Murphy, D. (Performer). (2017, March 27). Final Round. National Debate Tournament, Overland Park, Kansas.

Nave, N. (Performer). (2017, March 27). Final Round. National Debate Tournament, Overland Park, Kansas.

Sharpe, C. (2016). *In the Wake: On Blackness and Being*. Durham, NC: Duke University Press.

Warren, C. L. (2015). Black Nihilism and the Politics of Hope. *CR: The New Centennial Review, 15* (1), 215–248.

# 13

# MAKING THE WORLD GO DARK

## The Radical (Im)possibilities of Youth Organizing in the Afterlife of Slavery

*David C. Turner III*

## Introduction: Taking the Loss: LACOE Meeting

March 14, 2017

Following two months of organizing, research, classroom presentations, and teach-ins, a coalition of alumni and students at my old high school in the Inglewood Unified School District in Los Angeles County,[1] presented our case during the LA County Office of Education board meeting. The coalition of teachers, school administrators, youth, and community organizers came together to slow down the expansion of a charter school. A charter school network called Green Dot had made prior attempts to expand in the school district where Morningside high school resided. The network suggested that they will provide an alternative to traditional public schools. As the lead youth organizer and researcher on the Save Morningside campaign, it was my responsibility to conduct the research necessary to demonstrate why "We Say No to Green Dot" in our community. and more specifically, to give the youth ammunition to make their case about why they wanted to minimize charter schools in their district. After highlighting the profound ways that Green Dot reproduced anti-Black racism, both in their admissions practices and their disciplinary practices, we were confident that the LACOE board would vote in our favor to deny the petition to receive space in the Inglewood Unified School District. In one school, Locke, the Green Dot network suspended more students than the entire Inglewood Unified School District combined. At another school, Henry Clay, 2 out of every 3 Black students were suspended at least once. With the new climate towards restorative justice in the state of California, along with questionable admissions policies that created significant racial imbalances in schools (at high performing green dot schools, the African American population was below 15%), we knew we had the victory. Even the Inglewood Unified School District supported us.

We couldn't be more wrong.

Our hearts sank as the board voted 4-2 in favor of Green Dot. Their side of the room erupted in applause. We sat there, with anger boiling. Miesha, a student, said under her breath, "fuck it, they can all catch my fade outside right now if they think their coming to my hood with this shit." As we walked outside to our bus, the youth I rallied to come to the LACOE meeting were more angry than disappointed. They were ready to take this anger to drastic measures using direct action tactics and becoming "uncivil." One student, Jeffery, argued on the bus,

> "look yall, we took that L. Green Dot is trash, but I still don't know if I can go to college because my counselor hates me. Its people at the school and at they're main office [the district] that can get this work too. If anything, we should be fighting for our shit anyway, otherwise they're gonna take it in the same way that they just did [at the LACOE meeting]."

Miesha agreed, saying that, "look, if they really try and take over the school, we walking out everyday. Their test scores are gonna be trash fucking with us." The youth, even in their loss, were planning and justifying an uncivil politic that disrupts the civility imposed on them through public schools …

Losing anything hurts. As organizers, losing campaigns really hurts. Organizers are often thought of as community builders, who seek to, "an enduring network of people, who identify with common ideals and who can act on the basis of those ideals" (Stall & Stoecker, 1998, p. 730). For Black people, organizing takes on a deeper meaning, as we have traditionally sought to build community power in the interests of resource acquisition, community control, or political power (Jennings, 2000; Payne, 2007; Rustin, 1965). The moment you lose a campaign, you feel as if you put your heart, soul, and energy into something that will not change the conditions of your people. For Black organizers, we have an intimate knowledge of the sting of loss—when the state-sanctioned murderers of Black people (police) go free, when Black neighborhoods are gentrified and we are moved out, when pre-dominantly Black and Brown schools are closed, and when Black lives are just constantly under attack and sometimes it feels insurmountable.

Even though we know this feeling too well, I argue there is hope. Often times, because of the demands placed on us by neoliberal capitalism, which represented free market ideology and that all things must have solutions in the market (Harvey, 2005; Spence, 2015), we feel the need to see organizing as a transactional, market-based value rooted in our ability to deliver a product—the campaign victory. This pressure limits our political imaginations and pulls away from what our political possibilities can be. Learning from the youth at Morningside, politics can be a refusal to comply with something, or even an attempt to sabotage civil order. Sometimes, we as Black organizers need a new language to open our political possibilities, and it may be time to re-evaluate our political mission and goals. In this short chapter, I argue that a framework called Afropessimism helps organizers expand our political imaginations and possibilities by 1) providing a sharp critique of liberal organizing and 2) by embracing an uncivil politic to disrupt institutions invested in Black suffering. I support my argument by drawing on ethnographic field notes that I collected as a programs manager and a youth organizer for Urban Leaders Institute,[2] a community-based organization in Los Angeles during the 2016–2017 school year.

## Reorienting Ourselves: Moving Away from Liberal Organizing in the Afterlife of Slavery

One of the critical functions of Afropessimism is to collectively name and more precisely define anti-Blackness, which Dumas and ross (2016) define as "Rather, antiblackness refers to a broader antagonistic relationship between blackness and (the possibility of) humanity" (p. 429). Anti-Blackness, as it has been articulated, is the continued condition of slavery that not only denies Black humanity but positions Black people as the opposite of human—the anti-human who is fungible, killable, and not capable of suffering since they were once slaves (Dumas, 2013; Sexton, 2015). I frame my analysis of what happened at LACOE and the anti-Black dismal of legitimate claims through Saidiya Hartman's (2007) articulation of the afterlife of slavery. In the afterlife of slavery, Black people receive a "negative inheritance," being "skewed life chances, limited access to health and education, premature death, incarceration, and impoverishment" (Hartman, 2007 p. 6). Because of African enslavement and the political, cultural, social, and ideological infrastructure that grew from it, Black people in the United States and abroad have yet to fully become human in the wake of slavery (Sharpe, 2016). Many Black organizers have been trying to combat this inheritance through access to institutions, or through community autonomy and self-determination, especially in urban centers (Jennings, 2000). In the case of the Save Morningside campaign, the negative inheritance consists of how individual teachers, security guards, and some administrators will be blamed for poor Black student engagement at Green Dot, as opposed to the larger ideological and political implications of the larger structural failure to embrace and support Black children. The afterlife of slavery in this particular case is that the outcomes tied to Black students will be associated with an "individual prerogative" or failures of individual teachers, and not the state that facilitated this sanctioned suffering to begin with (Hartman, 1997). Losing that fight to Green Dot, in effect, suggested that it is OK for other charter school networks and all schooling entities to punish and disappear Black students for higher test scores, because Black suffering was not enough to deny a charter network access to a school district.

I opened with my experience at the LACOE school board for two reasons. First, as organizers, we are not measured on how effectively we can bring people out, or on the ways we politicize our communities, but we are often evaluated on our "wins" (Oakes, Rogers, & Lipton, 2006; Rogers & Morrell, 2011). We are evaluated and judged on which campaigns we participated in, and whether or not these campaigns brought about some sort of policy or practice related change in our communities. This is a larger historical shift in organizing in Black communities, as the growth of non-profits in the organizing world have begun to tie political goals and outcomes to funding (Kohl-Arenas, 2016; Kwon, 2013; Rodriguez, 2007; Tuck & Yang, 2014) What this meant for me at Morningside, was that I was legally unable to encourage their behavior to disrupt civility, and to be quite frank, it was my job to channel their righteous anger into something more "productive," which is getting involved in the political process the legal way with hopes of making incremental change. What this means, is that even though I have an understanding that the political logic that 21st-century community-based organizations adopt to civically challenge systems of power, I could not encourage the students to be uncivil, even though uncivility has helped to address the sociopolitical conditions of Black folks through riots and more direct challenges to the state (Bloom & Martin, 2013; Hooker, 2016; Sojoyner, 2013)This logic, rooted in schemas of discipline and self-governance, was established to control and limit the political autonomy of radical organizers (Rodriguez, 2007; Sojoyner, 2016). This shift has severely limited our political imagination, where policy wins become the bedrock for all things radical. Omi and Winant (2015) call this process *insulation*, where political energy becomes insulated into official structures, and no longer reflects the extent of the demands of social movement actors who are interested in liberation for their people.

Second, we organizers are often taught to inspire hope in young people and in our communities. Often, we know that the institutions we fight against have no regard for our lives and livelihood, but if we can just get them to *bend on this one issue*, then maybe we can get more. This model of organizing, the Alinsky model (1972), is often used as the go-to framework for community organizers (Speer & Hugher, 1995). We are taught to forgo our more radical politics in public spaces so we won't scare off potentials, and more specifically, we are trained not to paint our conditions as *hopeless* (Tuck & Yang, 2014). We see the world for what it is, then we mobilize the people, the only real resource we have, to fix it. Our strategies are often rooted in making people really mad about everything, and then focusing their energy into changing this *one little thing* that impacts them in some way. Indeed, it is a complicated transition to talk to youth about colonialism and white supremacy in one breath, and then tell them to use a democratic organizing process that their communities have never really had access to in another breath (see Kwon, 2013). Sometimes, it feels like we need a new language to help us frame what we want, and to then move the people in the directions they see fit towards liberation. But we get caught in the process asking, "What direction?"

## Afropessimism and the Use of Black Critique

As a political project, Afropessimism seeks to unmake the ways we understand race relations and racial power by arguing that African enslavement has never truly ended, and in the afterlife of slavery, Black folks have continued to be dispossessed and made fungible in order to maintain white wealth accumulation and satiable desire for Black suffering (Hartman, 1997; Tuck & Yang, 2014; Dumas, 2013). Afropessimism, as both a theoretical tradition and an analytic lens, can help organizers reframe what counts as a "win" or what to have "hope" in, by reframing how we understand race, racial power, and civil unrest. Discussing the Ferguson political moment, Minkah Makalani (2017) argues that the current formation of 21st century Black political resistance is largely unintelligible to the formal political establishment. Highlighting the centrality of anti-Black racism to the U.S. polity, Makalani argues, "to insist on a world where Black lives do matter brings into view those mechanisms by which Blackness continues to provide a baseline for a racialized US democracy, where Blackness remains visible as the point to which whites must never fall" (p. 534). The impact of Black Lives Matter, and specifically its broad understandings of state violence, leave technical and prescribed solutions such as body cameras or police education programs (which we may call organizing wins) void in addressing anti-Black violence. So, for us, a win could look like the burning of a police car, or a school walk-out for several days, because civil society relies on our cooperation in order to survive. Although this sounds like the rhetoric of many Black radicals who seek revolution, in academic fields like education, or in organizing circles, Afropessimism is painted as dogmatic fatalism that is not really useful for our people. In some spaces, it is seen as empty theorizing that does not help advance the conditions of Black people, and it has no real utility.

While I have certainly known the frustrations with academic and inaccessible language that is used to isolate organizers and those who do not have access to collegiate spaces, I actually believe that Afropessimism is an age-old reality for many Black folks. When activists like the Dream Defenders activate language like, "they never loved us," in response to Trayvon Martin (Davis, 2015), or when student organizers from California's public universities fought to force the University of California system to divest from private prisons (Williams,

2016), we are acutely aware of the ways that anti-Blackness operates in our communities to facilitate suffering. We hear pessimistic-like comments all the time from elders, from community members, and even from youth, who say things like, "They don't care about Black people; they never give a damn about us; they always trying to hold Black people back" and other colloquial sayings related to our conditions. Even though our jobs are to inspire hope, the condition of Blackness does not allow hopes to get too high.

So what do we do with this information?

As we continue organizing for social transformation and the liberation of Black people, it is important to remember that this nation cannot function with mass Black civil unrest and disturbance. Indeed, Black resistance of any kind, especially uncivil resistance, generates some of the greatest anxieties among white power structures (Bloom & Martin, 2013; Hooker, 2016; Makalani, 2017; Sojoyner, 2013). *It is our job, as organizers, to facilitate the type of political consciousness that leads to this type of uncivility.* Damien Sojoyner (2013, 2016) reminds us of the efforts to keep Black panthers, SNCC members, and radicalized gang members out of LAUSD schools, not for the sake of keeping kids safe, but to ensure that Black radicalism did not spoil Black students. In a paradoxical sense, it becomes our job as organizers to inspire chaos that disrupts whiteness at all costs, in every way possible.

## Embracing Uncivility in an (un)civil society: The Case of Social Justice High School

November 10, 2016

As walk-outs have been occurring all throughout the day, youth from SJHS in South Central Los Angeles joined thousands of students nationwide in protests regarding the results of the 2016 presidential election—the election of Donald Trump. One of our [the organization I work for] young people, Joaquin, helped to facilitate the walk out with a group of 3 other Latina students. Students left the school and marched down towards the University of Southern California. They tried to encourage students from a nearby high school, Traditional Public High School, to join them, however, the students TPHS were confronted with a rough choice: either walk out and be expelled or stay in school.

As the students were in the streets, they were chanting, "no justice, no peace!" and "fuck Donald Trump." More than once, the students were confronted by a trump supporter, typically a white male, who shouted back, "this is a democracy! If you don't like it, then get the fuck outta here." I can feel myself getting angry at this point, so I try and remind the heckler that these are minors, and he screamed back, "they should be in school where they belong."

The district and the assistant principals organized buses for the students to return to the campus. The main concern for the day was safety and being able to get the students back to school in a safe manner. In a conversation with some administrative staff, they were speaking about the nature of the event, and the amount of liabilities that they could potentially face since the students left school and walked. The students were encouraged to stay, yet they chose otherwise. Some of the administrative staff hinted at the possibility for teachers who participated in the walkout to be disciplined for their actions. Speaking to one of the assistant principals, she reminded me that no such thing would happen, but that the teachers needed to be reminded that they must "remain neutral" during these times, because they can incite political activity.

When I returned to the school, I waited in the office for my students. I spoke to my students about a demands process throughout the day, and their eyes began to light up. They started to realize that they had power, and that power could be exercised by a refusal, a refusal to be governed— they can refuse consent …

After these walk-outs, Joaquin and his Black leadership program teacher, Mr. R, were both "warned" about participating in any political activity around the election. They were specifically instructed not to organize anything again, for if they do, there would be serious disciplinary repercussions. In January of 2017, LAUSD put out a mandate, sternly stating that any administrator or LAUSD staff member that assisted youth during the walk-out will be terminated. This came following a plea, suggesting that youth in LAUSD schools stay in school, because the district needs them to be there. Organizing for (un)civility means being a bad citizen. It means breaking rules. It means not consenting to the demands placed on you by white civil society to make things happen. Even though these walk-outs did not have specific demands tied to them, the threat of not being able to control youth for a concentrated period of time presented an immense concern for school officials.

## Conclusion: Organizing Black Youth in the Afterlife of Slavery

The election of Barack Obama in 2008 brought about a large shift in the political lives of young Black people (Cohen, 2010). In some ways, his visibility as a Black organizer (or an organizer who happens to be Black) turned federal politician further legitimated policy-oriented organizing as a tool for political change. Even as the first Black president, who took classes with and publicly defended the late Derrick Bell, chose to condemn the uprisings in Baltimore and Ferguson, referring to both, especially to Baltimore, as "Thugs" who are not interested in justice. Fredrick Harris (Harris, 2012, 2014) highlights how Obama adopted respectability politics, which are "deliberate, highly self-conscious concession to hegemonic values" (Higginbotham, 1993), to win over white voters and condemn poor Black people for their own conditions. In this sense, President Obama adopted respectability politics to condemn the political imaginations and actions of Black youth who understood the power of destruction and uncivility to express discontent with a system designed for their demise (Ziyad, 2017)

Soo Ah Kwon (2013) asserts that young people, activists, and those interested in freedom need to become "bad citizens." By bad citizens, she does not mean that we should skip out on voting, or not pay taxes, she is implying that our forms of civic action simply will not disrupt power structures enough to transform our conditions. Kwon argues, "it may be that what we need are uncivil subjects, willing to inhabit bad citizenship in order to critique the supposed good faith of the state as a matter of governing ourselves" (p. 130). This uncivil subject, who one who would seek to "Make their test scores trash" like Miesha after the Save Morningside campaign, or like Joaquin, who helped to organize his student body to refuse being governed by school for a day, are what we may need. To be Black in the afterlife of slavery means to be considered the anti-human, and to not have your suffering be considered real or valid (Dumas, 2013; Sexton, 2015). This means that, presenting language of damage and deficit may not be the most effective strategy for organizing, especially if power structures refuse to acknowledge that damage in the first place (Tuck, 2009). In an advanced capitalist society, the state also needs subjects to play their role to maintain the white supremacist state of dominance and control. What Kwon is asking for, and what I hope to have demonstrated, is that we need to move beyond what the state views as action or activism for something more sustained, and radical. For us, "winning" a political campaign should not just consist of a policy victory, nor should maintaining hope mean that we continue to believe we can change a system that is structured to facilitate the literal and social death of Black people (Cacho, 2012; Hartman, 1997). We need to be willing to become "bad citizens," who are not supported by state-sanctioned institutions, to consistently combat anti-Blackness in all of its forms. As traditional organizing posits that we should be organizing for some sort of policy change; maybe, what we need to be organizing for is chaos.

## Notes

1 This campaign, and the results, are public information. They can be found in the minutes of the March 14 meeting here https://www.lacoe.edu/Portals/0/Board/No.%2024%20(3-14-17)%20Minutes.pdf.

Iam using real names of the school and of the campaign in order to demonstrate to other organizers that this type of framing, and this type of campaign, is real and happened in real life, with real people. The names of the youth who were identified in this field note were changed to protect their identity.

2 A pseudonym.

# References

Alinsky, S. D. (1972). *Rules for Radicals. October.* Retrieved from www.books4bestseller. com/rules-for-radicals.pdf.

Bloom, J., & Martin, W. E. (2013). *Black against Empire: The History and Politics of the Black Panther Party.* Berkeley, CA: University of California Press.

Cacho, L. M. (2012). *Social Death : Racialized Rightlessness and the Criminalization of the Unprotected.* New York: New York University Press. Retrieved from https:// nyupress.org/books/9780814723753/.

Cohen, C. J. (2010). *Democracy Remixed: Black Youth and the Future of American Politics.* New York: Oxford University Press.

Davis, C. H. F. (2015). "Dream Defending, On-Campus and Beyond: A Multi-Sited Ethnography of Contemporary Student Organizing, the Social Movement Repertoire, and Social Movement Organization in College." The University of Arizona. Retrieved from https://repository.arizona.edu/handle/10150/595672.

Dumas, M. J. (2013). 'Losing an arm': Schooling as a site of black suffering. *Race Ethnicity and Education, 17*(1), 1–29. https://doi.org/10.1080/13613324.2013.850412.

Dumas, M. J., & ross, k. m. (2016). "Be Real Black for Me" : Imagining BlackCrit in Education. *Urban Education, 51*(4), 415–442. https://doi.org/10.1177/0042085916628611.

Harris, F. C. (2012). *The Price of the Ticket : Barack Obama and the Rise and Decline of Black Politics.* Oxford: Oxford University Press.

Harris, F. C. (2014). The rise of respectability politics. *Dissent, 61*(1), 33–38. https://doi. org/10.1353/dss.2014.0010.

Hartman, S. (1997). *Scenes of Subjection: Terror, Slavery, and Self-Making in Nineteenth-Century America.* Oxford: Oxford University Press.

Hartman, S. (2007). *Lose Your Mother: A Journey along the Atlantic Slave Trade.* New York: Farrar, Straus, and Giroux.

Harvey, D. (2005). *A Brief History of Neoliberalism.* Oxford: Oxford University Press.

Higginbotham, E. B. (1993). *Righteous Discontent : The Women's Movement in the Black Baptist Church, 1880–1920.* Cambridge, MA: Harvard University Press. Retrieved from www.hup.harvard.edu/catalog.php?isbn=9780674769786.

Hooker, J. (2016). Black Lives Matter and the paradoxes of U.S. Black politics: From democratic sacrifice to democratic repair. *Political Theory,* 1–22. https://doi. org/10.1177/0090591716640314.

Jennings, J. (2000). *The Politics of Black Empowerment: The Transformation of Black Activism in Urban America.* Detroit, MI: Wayne State University Press.

Kohl-Arenas, E. (2016). *The Self-Help Myth: How Philanthropy Fails to Alleviate Poverty.* Berkeley, CA: University of California Press.

Kwon, S. A. (2013). *Uncivil Youth: Race, Activism, and Affirmative Governmentality.* Durham, NC: Duke University Press.

Makalani, M. (2017). Black Lives Matter and the limits of formal Black politics. *South Atlantic Quarterly, 116*(3), 529–552. https://doi.org/10.1215/00382876-3961472.

Oakes, J., Rogers, J., & Lipton, M. (2006). *Learning Power: Organizing for Education and Justice.* New York: Teachers College Press.

Omi, M. & Winant, H. (2015). *Racial Formations in the United States* (3rd ed.). New York: Routledge.

Payne, C. M. (2007). *I've Got the Light of Freedom: The Organizing Tradition of the Mississippi Freedom Struggle.* Berkeley, CA: University of California Press.

Rodriguez, D. (2007). The Political Logic of the Non-Profit Industrial Complex. In INCITE! Women of Color Against Violence (Eds.), *The Revolution Will Not be Funded: Beyond the Non-Profit Industrial Complex*. Boston, MA: South End Press.

Rogers, J., & Morrell, E. (2011). "A Force to be Reckoned With." The Campaign for College Access in Los Angeles. In M. Orr & J. Rogers (Eds.), *Public Engagement for Public Education: Joining Forces to Revitalize Democracy and Equalize Schools* (pp. 227–249). Stanford, CA: Stanford University Press.

Rustin, B. (1965). From protest to politics: The future of the civil rights movement. *League for Industrial Democracy, 39*(2), 25–31.

Sexton, J. (2015). Unbearable Blackness. *Cultural Critique, 90*(1), 159–178.

Sharpe, C. (2016). *In the Wake: On Blackness and Being*. Durham, NC: Duke University Press.

Sojoyner, D. M. (2013). Black radicals make for bad citizens: Undoing the myth of the school to prison pipeline. *Berkeley Review of Education, 4*(2), 241–263. Retrieved from http://escholarship.org/uc/item/35c207gv.

Sojoyner, D. M. (2016). *First Strike: Educational Enclosures in Black Los Angeles*. Minneapolis, MN: University of Minnesota Press.

Speer, P. W., & Hugher, J. (1995). Community organizing: An ecological route to empowerment and power. *American Journal of Community Psychology, 23*(5), 729–748.

Spence, L. K. (2015). *Knocking the Hustle: Against the Neoliberal Turn in Black Politics*. Brooklyn, NY: punctum books.

Stall, S., & Stoecker, R. (1998). COMMUNITY ORGANIZING OR ORGANIZING COMMUNITY?: Gender and the crafts of empowerment. *Gender & Society, 12*(6), 729–756. https://doi.org/10.1177/089124398012006008.

Tuck, E. (2009). Suspending damage: A letter to communities. *Harvard Educational Review, 79*(3), 409–428. https://doi.org/10.17763/haer.79.3.n0016675661t3n15.

Tuck, E., & Yang, K. W. (Eds.) (2014). *Youth Resistance Research and Theories of Change*. New York: Routledge.

Williams, A. J. (2016). The road to private prison divestment: Inside the University of California student campaign. *Boom: A Journal of California, 6*(2), 98–103. https://doi.org/10.1525/boom.2016.6.2.98.

Ziyad, H. (2017). Playing "outside" in the dark: Blackness in a postwhite world. *Critical Ethnic Studies, 3*(1), 143–161. https://doi.org/10.5749/jcritethnstud.3.1.0143.

# 14

# MORE THAN JUST POTENTIAL

Troubling Success Counternarratives in
Mathematics Education Research

*Erika C. Bullock*

Mathematics education research in the United States overflows with documentation of the "challenges" of educating Black children. Documentation of the
so-called Black–white achievement gap has led to hyperfocus on negativity
related to Black children in mathematics classrooms and an unrelenting quest
to find strategies that will "fix" Black children and acculturate them to school
mathematics. A reasonable way for education researchers to refute these claims
is to offer narratives that highlight Black students who are academically successful as proof that it is possible for Black children to excel in schools; I call
these efforts *success counternarratives*. In mathematics education research, the success counternarrative is a common methodological tool used to put forward an
alternate narrative of Black children's mathematical brilliance. However, there
remains a question of if success counternarratives are simply reactionary. Asked
differently, what do success counternarraties in mathematics education research
*do*? In this chapter, I trouble success counternarratives as a methodological approach in mathematics education research and consider how they appeal to
white benevolence and reify, albeit unintentionally, anti-blackness by limiting
the possibilities for Black agency in schools.

In a personal communication with Dreyfus and Rabinow (1983), Foucault
said: "People know what they do; frequently they know why they do what they
do; but what they don't know is what what they do does" (p. 187). I use this
quote as a template to structure this chapter according to three key questions:
*What do we do with success counternarratives? Why do we use success counternarratives?*
and *What do success counternarratives do?* I construct "we" as the set of mathematics education researchers concerned with Black children—including myself—
who are inclined to respond to discourses of deficiency (Berry, Ellis, & Hughes,

2014; Stinson, 2013) about Black children with stories that negate these discourses. Given the brevity of this chapter, I limit the scope of literature discussed to mathematics education—my domain of research—but I believe that the issues raised apply across domains of education research.

## What Do We Do with Success Counternarratives?

Much of success counternarrative research in mathematics education relies on the critical race methodology of counter-storytelling (e.g., Berry, 2008; Stinson, 2008; Thompson & Lewis, 2005). Counter-storytelling is the process of using research to establish narratives that oppose "majoritarian stories ... that carry layers of assumptions that persons in positions of racialized privilege bring with them to discussions of racism, sexism, classism, and other forms of subordination" (Solórzano & Yosso, 2002, p. 28). Critical race counternarratives center marginalized experience to exploit fissures in the majoritarian stories and to create new ways of seeing. Although critical race counter-storytelling is a common methodology for success counternarrative studies in mathematics education, there exist success counternarrative studies in that do not use critical race counter-storytelling (e.g., McGee & Martin, 2011, described below).

Mathematics education researchers use success counternarratives to disrupt the majoritarian narrative that Black students are mathematically deficient and thus relegated to inferior performance. Berry, Ellis, and Hughes (2014) summarize Black students' experiences in mathematics as follows:

> Black learners in mathematics experience the following conditions: (a) reduced access to advanced mathematics courses that prepare them for higher education and improved career options; (b) routine exposure to activities that focus primarily on rote, decontextualized learning through drill and practice with little to no engagement in activities that promote reasoning and position mathematics as a tool to analyze social and economic issues, critique power dynamics, and build advocacy; and (c) less access to qualified teachers of mathematics who both understand mathematics deeply and understand their students' cultural and community context deeply in order to give learners access to mathematical knowledge. (p. 541)

Success counternarratives do not deny these conditions. Rather, they focus on those Black students who persist in mathematics within them. For example, McGee and Martin (2011) introduce *stereotype management* stereotype threat as a tool to understand how successful Black mathematics students negotiate mathematics classrooms. I classify this study as a success counternarrative because the authors not only highlight successful students but they show that these students must engage in a series of psychosocial moves to gain and maintain their success. This story of extra-mathematical work for successful Black students operates as a success counternarrative.

## Why Do We Use Success Counternarratives?

As a former mathematics teacher and current mathematics education researcher who is concerned with Black children, I am familiar with the urge to defend Black children amidst discourses of deficiency. Many of my students and I are exceptions to these discourses, and most research does not reflect our experiences. Success counternarratives present compelling discursive exceptions. They inject doubt and nuance into dominant narratives about Black students in mathematics. In their case study of a successful Black male high school mathematics student, Thompson and Lewis (2005) assert that the counternarrative is important because it "allows [the researchers] to contribute to a deeper understanding of African American mathematics achievement by offering a detailed examination of success to augment the many examinations of failure" (pp. 7–8). For Berry, Thunder, and McClain (2011), "counter narratives provide alternative lenses of analyses [*sic*] and interpretations of the experiences of African American students as mathematics learners" (p. 11). In her investigation of successful Black students' peer groups, Walker (2006) chooses to rebut an assumption about successful Black mathematics students: that they do not have an academic community. The success counternarrative calls upon the reader to see the story of Black children in mathematics as more than one of failure. Black children are capable of mathematical excellence and those who achieve this excellence do so in ways that defy common thinking about their academic resources.

## What Do Success Counternarratives Do?

Using afro-pessimism as an analytical lens to problematize success counternarratives as a methodological strategy to undermine discourses of deficiency about Black students in mathematics, I ask the following question: is it possible that success counternarratives unintentionally reinscribe anti-blackness as endemic to the system of mathematics education research? My affirmative response has led me to consider success counternarratives as dangerous (cf. Foucault, 1983) and, thus, requiring us to consider alternative disruptive methodological action. I position this question as a methodological one based on the understanding that decisions about how a researcher will respond to research questions are methodological choices. Methodological questions get to the *why* of research decision-making, grounded in "the values, attitudes and beliefs of the researcher who has made the choices" (Burton, 2001, p. 171). It is important to note that I am not arguing that researchers who employ success counternarratives reify anti-blackness *with intention*. In fact, my position is that the insidious nature of anti-blackness places us in a methodological conundrum. On the one hand, stories of Black success in mathematics are necessary for the historical and intellectual record. On the other hand, however, afropessimism reveals within these methodological decisions a dangerous tacit alignment with anti-blackness. In this section, I explore two areas where this alignment becomes visible.

### Success Counternarratives Minimize Black Suffering in Schools

Dumas (2013) describes Black suffering as one product of schooling "that we have been least willing or able to acknowledge or give voice to in educational scholarship" (p. 2). Counternarratives of Black students' success in mathematics elevate Black students' resilience amidst structures—as outlined in Berry, Ellis, and Hughes (2014) above—that are dedicated to impeding their progress. Success counternarratives suggest that all Black students have the potential to succeed in mathematics if the appropriate conditions are met—if teachers overcome racist beliefs, if schools and communities provide out-of-school support resources, if mathematics tasks address issues relevant to the students' communities, and so on. These stories imply that if schools can just see Black students as potential exceptions to the rules that dominant narratives have set for them, then they will create possibilities for more students to excel. I will return to this idea in the concluding section.

While the conditions that these studies highlight are important, meeting them does not remediate the psychic violence that students experience in schools. Black students who are successful in mathematics are not exempt from this violence. Mathematics education research that features success counternarratives does not address the potential expenses that the focal students may incur for their success. Martin and McGee (2009) liken achievement in school mathematics to a process of assimilation to a "mathematics literacy for African Americans based on the well-being of White children" (p. 209). Achievement has been constructed as white property (Ispa-Landa & Conwell, 2014; Ladson-Billings & Tate, 1995) and accessing that property can require some level of cultural compromise for Black students.

Successful Black mathematics students are also susceptible to the larger violent conditions in schools. For example, mathematics success does not eradicate the inextricable link between schools and prisons that is steeped in anti-blackness (Wun, 2016b). Mathematics achievement does not render Black girls immune to disproportionate discipline and encounters with law enforcement in the name of what adults perceive as bad attitudes, insubordination, or defiance (Morris, 2016; Wun, 2016a; 2016b). Excellence in school mathematics does not restore the innocence that anti-blackness strips from Black children when it positions them as "guilty subjects who warrant punishment" (Wun, 2016b, p. 744).

## Success Counternarratives Promote Normative Notions of Academic Success

Wynter (2006) argues that it is not possible to address the issue of consciousness from a Western rationality. She challenges Western understandings of what is normal: "WE WANT TO BUY INTO 'NORMALCY,' AS 'NORMALCY' IS CONSIDERED WITHIN THE VERY TERMS OF THE VERY ORDER OF 'KNOWLEDGE' WHICH HAS MADE US 'DEVIANT!'" (p. 3, capitalization original). For Sexton (2011), normativity is about "whose being is the generative force, historic occasion, and essential byproduct of the question of human being in general" (p. 7). This normative sense of humanity centers whiteness, rendering blackness deviant and pathological. In mathematics education, normativity is established in discussions about the Black-white achievement gap, where Black children are assigned value through their proximity to white student achievement (Gutiérrez, 2008). Therefore, white students define normalcy in the mathematics classroom, and Black students become deviant.

Mathematics education researchers most often address achievement in one of two ways: performance on standardized tests or affective response to mathematics (i.e., feeling "good," "capable," or "interested"). Although Robert Moses' (Moses & Cobb, 2002) charge to take on access to mathematics as a civil rights issue has become central to discussions connecting mathematics and social justice (Larnell, Bullock, & Jett, 2016), use of mathematics as a social tool is not a normative (i.e., white, middle-class) measure of success or achievement. The reverential space that mathematics occupies in Western culture positions mathematics as the greatest of intellectual endeavors, so mathematical success is signaled by measures that reflect intellect rather than social commitment (Ladson-Billings, 1997). For example, Woolley, Strutchens, Gilbert, and Martin (2010) use grades in mathematics classes, hours spent working on mathematics outside of class, and SAT mathematics scores as measures of mathematics outcomes. Other researchers point to enrollment in higher-level mathematics courses (McGee & Pearman, 2015), selection of mathematics-intensive majors (Ellington & Frederick, 2010; Jett, 2010), peer or teacher assessment (Walker, 2006), or, of course, standardized test scores (Berry et al., 2011) as success measures. Stiff and Harvey (1988) describe these indicators as European cultural products that "Black students must accept ... or become identified as unwilling or unable to 'cooperate'" (p. 198).

Ladson-Billings (1995) established academic success or academic achievement as one of three pillars of culturally relevant pedagogy. In doing so, she urged readers to consider the idea of academic success in broader-than-normative terms. Shifting the terms of success also interrupts the use of achievement as a tool "to socially construct Black children as deficient in service to dominant racial ideologies that render Black culture, families, and communities as pathological" (D. B. Martin, 2011, p. 446). Martin and McGee (2009) argue that changing the boundaries of success for Black students in mathematics requires "challenging the very education system in which school mathematics is learned and reshaping the opportunity structure in which it is argued that African Americans must participate" (p. 208). They maintain that success for Black students in mathematics is inextricably linked to their ability to use mathematics to evaluate and change the conditions in their lives and communities— or their development of sociopolitical consciousness (Ladson-Billings, 1995). The rising discourse of teaching and learning mathematics for social justice (TLMSJ) uses this idea of using mathematics to achieve sociopolitical aims, but the mainstream elements of this discourse in the United States have not risen to the point of challenging notions of achievement in these terms (Larnell et al., 2016).

## No Humans Involved

In the aftermath of the 1991 Rodney King beating in Los Angeles reports indicated that law enforcement in Los Angeles used the acronym NHI (No Humans Involved) when reporting situations where they used violence against Black men who lived in the cities impoverished areas. These men were not white, middle-class, or educated and they lived in the wrong places, so they could be treated as something other than human. Violent acts against them that would not be fathomable toward others or in other parts of town were justified because these men were disposable and possessed some animalistic nature that warranted excessive force (Wynter, 1994). Mathematics education for Black children has functioned according to a similar logic. Black students are treated as expendable in mathematics curriculum and policy because, despite increased rhetorical attention to equity, these documents are still constructed based on a white rationality that is inherently anti-Black and promotes a mythology of mathematics as white and male (D. B. Martin, 2015; Stinson, 2013).

Success counternarratives in mathematics education research rely on the possibility of creating something new: a new way of seeing Black students as *potentially* exceptional rather than inherently incapable. The implied message is that Black children are worthy of investment and equal treatment in schools because they have the potential to be successful mathematics students. While these studies bring forward important narratives, they encourage a response to Black students that is based on their potential rather than on their humanity. When it comes to Black students in mathematics, there are no humans involved. Success counternarratives dehumanize successful students by holding them up as exceptions to dominant racial narratives while failing to fully acknowledge the consequences of their exceptionality and their continued susceptibility to those same narratives.

Considering success counternarratives through the lens of afro-pessimism reveals a conflict that Moten (2008) describes as "strife between normativity and the deconstruction of norms [that] is essential ... to contemporary black academic discourse" (p. 178). This conflict creates the methodological challenge for mathematics education researchers who focus on Black children that I address in this chapter. I am not convinced that success counternarratives have no value in the corpus of mathematics education research about Black children, but I do think that the issue warrants some re-thinking. Martin (as cited in Gholson, Bullock, & Alexander, 2012) argues that an approach to mathematics education research for Black children must begin with an axiom:[1] "Black children are brilliant." Taking this idea as axiomatic means that it would no longer be the mathematics education researchers' work to *prove* that Black children can be successful in mathematics. Rather, any examination of why Black students are not performing as desired in mathematics *must* turn toward the structure of schools or of school mathematics. There is nothing to "fix" about the children. I call upon Martin's proposition as a starting point for this re-thinking. What is the role of success counternarratives in mathematics education research when we accept the axiom that Black children are brilliant? What methodological choices become possible or impossible under these conditions?

## Note

1  "An *axiom* is a logical statement that is assumed to be true. Axioms are not proven or demonstrated, but rather considered to be self-evident. Axioms serve as starting points for deducing and inferring other truths" (Gholson et al., 2012, p. 2).

## References

Berry, R. Q., III. (2008). Access to upper-level mathematics: The stories of successful African American middle school boys. *Journal for Research in Mathematics Education, 39*(5), 464–488.

Berry, R. Q., III, Ellis, M. W., & Hughes, S. (2014). Examining a history of failed reforms and recent stories of success: Mathematics education and Black learners of mathematics in the United States. *Race Ethnicity and Education, 17*(4), 540–568.

Berry, R. Q., III, Thunder, K., & McClain, O. L. (2011). Counter narratives: Examining the mathematics and racial identities of black boys who are successful with school mathematics. *Journal of African American Males in Education, 2*(1), 10–23.

Burton, L. (2001). Confounding methodology and methods. *British Journal of Sociology of Education, 22*(1), 171–175.

Dreyfus, H. L., & Rabinow, P. (1983). *Michel Foucault: Beyond structuralism and hermeneutics* (2nd ed.). Chicago, IL: The University of Chicago Press.

Dumas, M. J. (2013). "Losing an arm": Schooling as a site of black suffering. *Race Ethnicity and Education, 17*(1), 1–29.

Ellington, R. M., & Frederick, R. (2010). Black high achieving undergraduate mathematics majors discuss success and persistence in mathematics. *The Negro Educational Review, 61*(1–4), 61–84.

Foucault, M. (1983). On the genealogy of ethics: An overview of work in progress. In *Michel Foucault: Beyond structuralism and hermeneutics* (pp. 229–252). Chicago, IL: The University of Chicago Press.

Gholson, M. L., Bullock, E. C., & Alexander, N. N. (2012). On the brilliance of Black children: A response to a clarion call. *Journal of Urban Mathematics Education*, *5*(1), 1–7.

Gutiérrez, R. (2008). A "gap-gazing" fetish in mathematics education? Problematizing research on the achievement gap. *Journal for Research in Mathematics Education*, *39*(4), 357–364.

Ispa-Landa, S., & Conwell, J. (2014). "Once you go to a white school, you kind of adapt": Black adolescents and the racial classification of schools. *Sociology of Education*, *88*(1), 1–19.

Jett, C. C. (2010). "Many are called, but few are chosen": The role of spirituality and religion in the educational outcomes of "chosen" African American male mathematics majors. *The Journal of Negro Education*, *79*(3), 324–334.

Ladson-Billings, G. (1995). But that's just good teaching!: The case for culturally relevant pedagogy. *Theory Into Practice*, *34*(3), 159–165.

Ladson-Billings, G. (1997). It doesn't add up: African American students' mathematics achievement. *Journal for Research in Mathematics Education*, *28*(6), 697–708.

Ladson-Billings, G., & Tate, W. F., IV. (1995). Toward a critical race theory of education. *Teachers College Record*, *97*(1), 47–68.

Larnell, G. V., Bullock, E. C., & Jett, C. C. (2016). Rethinking teaching and learning mathematics for social justice from a critical race perspective. *The Journal of Education*, *196*(1), 19–29.

Martin, D. B. (2011). What does quality mean in the context of white institutional space? In B. Atweh, M. Graven, W. Secada, & P. Valero (Eds.), *Mapping equity and quality in mathematics education* (pp. 437–450). Dordrecht: Springer.

Martin, D. B. (2015). The collective black and *Principles to Actions. Journal of Urban Mathematics Education*, *8*(1), 17–23.

Martin, D. B., & McGee, E. O. (2009). Mathematics literacy and liberation: Reframing mathematics education for African-American children. In B. Greer, S. Mukhopadhyay, A. B. Powell, & S. Nelson-Barber (Eds.), *Culturally responsive mathematics education* (pp. 207–238). New York, NY: Routledge.

McGee, E. O., & Martin, D. B. (2011). "You would not believe what I have to go through to prove my intellectual value!" Stereotype management among academically successful black mathematics and engineering students. *American Educational Research Journal*, *48*(6), 1347–1389.

McGee, E. O., & Pearman, F. A., III. (2015). Understanding black male mathematics high schievers from the inside out: Internal risk and protective factors in high school. *The Urban Review*, *47*, 513–540.

Morris, M. W. (2016). *Pushout: The criminalization of Black girls in schools*. New York, NY: The New Press.

Moses, R. P., & Cobb, C. E. (2002). Radical equations: Civil rights from Mississippi to the Algebra Project. Boston, MA: Beacon Press.

Moten, F. (2008). The case of blackness. *Criticism*, *50*(2), 177–218.

Sexton, J. (2011). The social life of social death: On afro-pessimism and Black optimism. *InTensions*, *5*, 1–47.

Solórzano, D. G., & Yosso, T. J. (2002). Critical race methodology: Counter-storytelling as an analytical framework for education research. *Qualitative Enquiry*, *8*(1), 23–44.

Stiff, L. V., & Harvey, W. B. (1988). On the education of black children in mathematics. *Journal of Black Studies*, *19*(2), 190–203.

Stinson, D. W. (2008). Negotiating sociocultural discourses: The counter-storytelling of academically (and mathematically) successful African American male students. *American Educational Research Journal, 45*(4), 975–1010.

Stinson, D. W. (2013). Negotiating the "white male math myth": African American male students and success in school mathematics. *Journal for Research in Mathematics Education, 44*(1), 69–99.

Thompson, L. R., & Lewis, B. F. (2005). Shooting for the stars: A case study of the mathematics achievement and career attainment of an African American high school student. *The High School Journal, 88*(4), 6–18.

Walker, E. N. (2006). Urban high school students' academic communities and their effects on mathematics success. *American Educational Research Journal, 43*(1), 41–71.

Woolley, M. E., Strutchens, M. E., Gilbert, M. C., & Martin, W. G. (2010). Mathematics success of black middle school students: Direct and indirect effects of teacher expectations and reform practices. *The Negro Educational Review, 61*(1–4), 41–59.

Wun, C. (2016a). Against captivity: Black girls and school discipline policies in the afterlife of slavery. *Educational Policy, 30*(1), 171–196.

Wun, C. (2016b). Unaccounted foundations: Black girls, anti-black racism, and punishment in schools. *Critical Sociology, 42*(4–5), 737–750.

Wynter, S. (1994). "No humans involved": An open letter to my colleagues. *Forum N. H. I. Knowledge for the St Century, 1*(1), 42–73.

Wynter, S. (2006). *Proud Flesh* inter/views: Sylvia Wynter. *Proud Flesh: New Afrikan Journal of Culture, Politics and Consciousness, 4*, 1–36.

# INDEX

For Product Safety Concerns and Information please contact our EU
representative GPSR@taylorandfrancis.com
Taylor & Francis Verlag GmbH, Kaufingerstraße 24, 80331 München, Germany